In Praise

of Mothers

In Praise of Mothers

A Literary Anthology

Edited by Lilly Golden

THE ATLANTIC MONTHLY PRESS
NEW YORK

for my mother

Published simultaneously in Canada
Printed in the United States of America

FIRST EDITION

Library of Congress Cataloging-in-Publication Data

In praise of mothers: a literary anthology / edited by Lilly Golden.—1st ed.
ISBN 0-87113-569-8
1. Mothers—Literary collections. I. Golden, Lilly.
PN6071.M716 1994
808.83'1083520432—dc20 93-43223

DESIGN BY LAURA HOUGH

The Atlantic Monthly Press
841 Broadway
New York, NY 10003

10 9 8 7 6 5 4 3 2 1

Contents

Contents

Introduction

Lilly Golden

In Praise of Mothers is a collection of fourteen unforgettable stories about mothers and motherhood by some of the finest writers of our century.

Hundreds of stories of outstanding literary merit and emotional complexity are necessarily omitted from this collection. One reason is that all such stories cannot possibly fit within the bindings of one volume. But another is that *In Praise of Mothers* attempts to be what its title suggests—a celebration of maternity in all its forms. This distinction does not imply the automatic exclusion of stories involving anger and disappointment—because if it is honesty we require from literary fiction, what worthy story could deny the difficulties inherent within all mother-child bonds?—but favors stories tempered by love and respect. They are laudatory without being sentimental, revelatory without being unkind; and each explores, in its own way, the universal truths and mysteries of motherhood.

Women become mothers for the first time in the opening two stories of this collection, "The Shepherd's Wife" by William Maxwell and "Another Marvelous Thing" by Laurie Colwin. The former takes place in a mythical village in Bohemia and the latter in a modern urban hospital. In Maxwell's story a midwife, roused from her hovel in the night, presides over a difficult delivery in a couple's bedroom. In Colwin's, the obstetrician performs a cesarean section in a sterile operating room and the infant is whisked away to the high-tech neonatal intensive care unit. Radically different in setting and style, the two stories are, remarkably, the same tale of new motherhood, premature birth, hope, fear, pain, and the miracle of life.

What it means to be a mother—spiritually, emotionally, and, particularly, legally—is challenged in Bertolt Brecht's "The Augsburg Chalk Circle." The story poses the age-old (and timely) question of whether an adoptive mother has a greater or lesser claim to a child than has the biological mother. The story begins when a baby, abandoned by its mother, is retrieved by a caring servant. It ends several years later in a court of law where a judge, in the spirit of King Solomon, brilliantly determines the rightful mother of the child.

The mothers and daughters in Jane Goodall's "Mothers and Daughters" (the only piece of nonfiction in the book) are chimpanzees. Her exploration of their relationships illuminates with surprising clarity the roles played by "nature" and "nurture"—and an utterly haunting parallel to human behavior emerges.

One of the stories featuring mothers and sons is Frank O'Connor's "My Oedipus Complex," which hilariously chronicles a young boy's reluctance to share his mother with his father, just returned from war. But in "Women and Children First," by Francine Prose, a single mother's son has her all to himself—whether he likes it or not.

Some mothers in these stories show amazing strength, both physical and metaphysical. In Louise Erdrich's story "The Leap," a mother heroically saves her daughter's life. It is followed by David Leavitt's "Gravity," in which a mother, no less heroically, stands by her slowly dying son, helpless to rescue him.

In Alice Walker's "Everyday Use," a mother defends herself and her culture against her sophisticated, visiting daughter. Two mothers in "Groom Service" by Michael Dorris orchestrate a match between one's son and the other's daughter. The young man must undergo trials of patience and humility—in the tradition of his people—to gain the hand that his mother has forced upon him. The story opens with a pact between two mothers and closes with the birth of their first (shared) grandchild.

With age some mothers have more to teach their children than ever. In "Fenstad's Mother," by Charles Baxter, a middle-aged man still has much to learn from his politically and intellectually progressive, aging mother—if he is clever enough to notice. An indefatigable mother in Mary Lavin's "Happiness" indoctrinates her three daughters with her own stubborn refusal to be unhappy. Hortense Calisher's "Songs My Mother Taught Me" is a reminiscence of the lessons taught by her mother and their amusing applications years after she is gone.

In the final story, Pearl S. Buck's "The Good Deed,"

an old woman, unwillingly uprooted from her life in China by her Americanized son, finds purpose in a strange new land when she is needed for the first time in a long while.

In this collection are new mothers, mothers with young children, single mothers of children who are struggling toward adulthood, aging mothers of middle-aged children, and mothers remembering their own mothers. Some are married, some widowed, and some divorced. They are of many cultures and countries. They are wise, controlling, noble, vulnerable, kind, wishful, brave, and inconsistent. You may recognize your mother among them. You may also recognize yourself. These beautiful stories are collected in honor of all mothers and their children, and since mothers are also the children of their own mothers, the voices, rising from these pages in a chorus of praise, are especially for you.

The Shepherd's Wife

William Maxwell

There was a shepherd's wife in Bohemia who was greatly saddened when, after twelve years of being married, she still had no children. Her husband was a quiet man, large and slow-moving and dependable, and she loved him with all her heart, but he had no gift for speech, perhaps from spending so much time with animals, and instead of the prattle of childish voices that she so longed to hear, the woman was forced to be content with the ticking of the clock and the sound of the teakettle on the crane, the singing of wet wood on the hearth. Sometimes her husband was gone for days at a time, and then the sound of her own footsteps grew unbearably loud, and she thought that if only her husband would come home, so she could hear his heavy sigh when he sat down and warmed himself before the fire, and the dog's tail thumping, she wouldn't ask for more—not even the children that had been denied her.

For every deprivation there is always some gift, and the shepherd's wife was famous throughout the village for her ability to make things grow. The windows of her cottage were full of flowering plants all winter long, and when other women had trouble with their house plants—the leaves turning yellow and dropping off and no new green coming, or red spider, or white fly, or mealy bug, or aphids—when their favorite plants were, in fact, almost ready to be thrown on the compost heap, they would bring them to the shepherd's wife and say, "Can you do anything with this? It used to have masses of blooms and now look at it!" and the shepherd's wife would make a place for the sick plant on the windowsill on the south side of the kitchen, where the sun poured in all day long through the thick, round glass. A month later she would wrap the plant up carefully against the cold and deliver it to its owner, in full leaf, with new buds forming all over it.

"What ever do you do to make things grow?" the other women asked her. "Do you water them very often, or just every other day, or what is your secret?"

"To make plants grow," the shepherd's wife always said, "you have to look at them every day. If you forget about them or neglect them, they die."

The other women, whose households were blessed with children, never remembered this advice or quite believed in it, and there was even a rumor (for it was a very small place, and no one living there escaped the breath of slander) that the shepherd's wife was a witch.

Actually, there was more to it than she could ever quite bring herself to tell them. After all, they had their little Josephs and Johns and Mary Catherines, and she had only her Christmas cactus, her climbing geraniums, her white rosebush in its big tub, and her pink oleander. So she kept her secret, which was that she not only looked at every plant every day but also talked to them, the way some lonely people talk to animals or to themselves.

"Now," she would say, standing in front of the Christmas cactus, when the shepherd was out of the house and there was nobody around to hear her, "I know you're slow by nature, but so is my husband, and he has his happy moments and you should have yours. All you need to do is grow a little." Then she would pass on to the pink oleander. "What is *this?*" she would exclaim. "Why are your leaves dry and stiff this morning? Too much sun? Very well, behind the curtain you go until you are feeling better." Then, to the white rosebush: "Just because those great geraniums are almost touching the ceiling and crowding everything else out, you needn't think I don't know you are here. Besides, if you will notice, the geranium blossom has no scent. . . ." So she talked to the plants, as if they were children, and, like children, they grew and grew and blossomed over and over again all winter long.

One day, the old midwife who always took care of the birth of children in the village came to the shepherd's wife and, drawing her to the chimney corner where the kettle was boiling for tea, said, "It's time somebody told you—you are with child."

At first the woman wouldn't believe it, although the

midwife had never been known to make a mistake in these matters, and when she did believe that it was true, she was still not happy. "I've waited too long," she told herself. "If children had come when I was younger, it would have been very different. Now I don't know what will happen to me. I may die. And if nothing dreadful happens to me, something will certainly happen to my Christmas cactus, my climbing geraniums, my rosebush, and my pink oleander as soon as I take to my bed and cannot look at them and talk to them the way they are used to."

She didn't confide these fears to her husband, not wanting to spoil his happiness, but he knew her moods, and when he saw that in spite of the blessing that had come to them she was still heavy-hearted, he stayed home with her more, and arranged with the other shepherds to mind his flocks for him. Wherever she went about the cottage, scrubbing and cleaning and putting things in order, he watched her, hoping to find out what was on her mind.

Having him around the house so much made her nervous, and when the plants began to drop their leaves and turn yellow because she couldn't bring herself to talk to them in front of anybody, she saw the fulfillment of her worst fears. She became pale, her shoulders drooped, she never spoke of the future, never discussed with her husband what they might name the child, or even whether it was going to be a boy or a girl. It was as if the child inside her were somebody else's plant that she could care for with her body but must not become attached to.

When her time came, the shepherd ran through the snowy night to the poor hovel that was all the midwife had for a roof over her head, and brought her hobbling back across the ice and snow. He put the kettle on the crane and built up a roaring fire and tried to stop his ears against the sounds that came from the bedroom—sounds that made his heart stop with terror. He felt a desperate need to talk to someone, but the midwife was too busy, coming and going with her hot cloths and her basins of boiling water, and she would not listen to him. At last he turned to the plants and told them his fears. Immediately before his eyes the limp leaves began to straighten, the stems to turn green. He went on talking to them without perceiving that anything unnatural had happened. His wife's secret was safe. He was a man, and so it didn't interest him.

In the terrible course of time, while the shepherd sat with his head in his hands and cursed the day he was born, the moans in the next room became screams and cries, and then suddenly there were two cries instead of one. A little while later, the midwife appeared with a baby, the smallest that had ever been seen in the village. She removed the soft woolen scarves it was wrapped in, and showed it to the shepherd, who sprang up with such pride in his heart and such happiness in his face that the newborn babe responded and began to wave its arms feebly.

"You have a daughter," the old midwife said.

"From God," the shepherd said.

"A very small, meachin, puny daughter," the old midwife said scornfully.

"She will be the most beautiful and proud woman that ever lived," the shepherd said. "She will be as beautiful and proud as the forests of Bohemia."

When the old midwife left him to care for the mother and child, he turned again to the plants on the windowsill, and when the sun came up and lighted their leaves, he was still telling them about his newborn daughter.

* * *

Day after day the plants grew, but the baby did not, and the mother remained feverish and pale on her bed and did not love her child. When the shepherd knelt beside her and asked how she was feeling, she shook her head and did not say what she thought, which was, I shall never get up out of this bed.

She didn't dare ask about the plants—if they had died one by one, and been thrown out—but one day, after the midwife had gone to assist at the birth of another child, and the man had left the house for a few minutes to see about his sheep, the woman got up out of bed, intending to get back in again as soon as she had satisfied her curiosity. She tottered into the kitchen expecting to see the dry stalks of all her beloved plants, or maybe nothing at all, and what met her eyes was a green bower of blossoms such as she, who was famous throughout the village for her ability to make things grow, had never managed to have. The scent of the flowers was heavy in the low-ceilinged room, and as she stood there, looking at her Christmas cactus, her climbing geraniums, her white rosebush, and her pink oleander, the tight center of her heart opened, petal by petal.

She ran into the bedroom, where the child fretted, and brought it, cradle and all, into the room where the flowers were. "This is my very own daughter," she said. "She's very small, and she cries all the time, but some of you were sickly too, at first, and dropped your leaves, and showed every sign of not flourishing, and now look at you. Dearest heart," she said, pulling back the woolen cover until she could see the shadowy silken skin at the baby's throat. "Now you must grow. You must stop fretting. You must sleep," she said, unbuttoning her dress and helping the tiny pale mouth to find her breast. "You must grow tall and proud and beautiful, like the forests of Bohemia."

Another Marvelous Thing

Laurie Colwin

On a cold, rainy morning in February, Billy Delielle stood by the window of her hospital room looking over Central Park. She was a week and a half from the time her baby was due to be born, and she had been put into the hospital because her blood pressure had suddenly gone up and her doctor wanted her constantly monitored and on bed rest.

A solitary jogger in bright red foul-weather gear ran slowly down the glistening path. The trees were black and the branches were bare. There was not another soul out. Billy had been in the hospital for five days. The first morning she had woken to the sound of squawking. Since her room was next door to the nursery, she assumed this was a sound some newborns made. The next day she got out of bed at dawn and saw that the meadow was full of sea gulls who congregated each morning before the sun came up.

The nursery was an enormous room painted soft yellow. When Billy went to take the one short walk a day allowed her, she found herself averting her eyes from the neat rows of babies in their little plastic bins, but once in a while she found herself hungry for the sight of them. Taped to each crib was a blue I'M A BOY or pink I'M A GIRL card telling mother's name, the time of birth, and birth weight.

At six in the morning the babies were taken to their mothers to be fed. Billy was impressed by the surprising range of noises they made: mewing, squawking, bleating, piping, and squealing. The fact that she was about to have one of these creatures herself filled her with a combination of bafflement, disbelief, and longing.

For the past two months her chief entertainment had been to lie in bed and observe her unborn child moving under her skin. It had knocked a paperback book off her stomach and caused the saucer of her coffee cup to jiggle and dance.

Billy's husband, Grey, was by temperament and inclination a naturalist. Having a baby was right up his street. Books on neonatology and infant development replaced the astronomy and bird books on his night table. He gave up reading mysteries for texts on childbirth. One of these books had informed him that babies can hear in the womb, so each night he sang "Roll Along Kentucky Moon" directly into Billy's stomach. Another suggested that the educational process could begin before birth. Grey thought he might try to teach the unborn to count.

"Why stop there?" Billy said. "Teach it fractions."

Billy had a horror of the sentimental. In secret, for she would rather have died than showed it, the thought of her own baby brought her to tears. Her dreams were full of infants. Babies appeared everywhere. The buses abounded with pregnant women. The whole process seemed to her one half miraculous and the other half preposterous. She looked around her on a crowded street and said to herself: "Every single one of these people was *born.*"

Her oldest friend, Penny Stern, said to her: "We all hope that this pregnancy will force you to wear maternity clothes, because they will be so much nicer than what you usually wear." Billy went shopping for maternity clothes but came home empty-handed.

She said, "I don't wear puffed sleeves and frilly bibs and ribbons around my neck when I'm not pregnant, so I don't see why I should have to just because I am pregnant." In the end, she wore Grey's sweaters, and she bought two shapeless skirts with elastic waistbands. Penny forced her to buy one nice black dress, which she wore to teach her weekly class in economic history at the business school.

Grey set about renovating a small spare room that had been used for storage. He scraped and polished the floor, built shelves, and painted the walls pale apple green with the ceiling and moldings glossy white. They had once called this room the lumber room. Now they referred to it as the nursery. On the top of one of the shelves Grey put his collection of glass-encased bird's nests. He already had in mind a child who would go on nature hikes with him.

As for Billy, she grimly and without expression submitted herself to the number of advances science had come up with in the field of obstetrics.

It was possible to have amniotic fluid withdrawn and analyzed to find out the genetic health of the unborn and, if you wanted to know, its sex. It was possible to lie on a table and with the aid of an ultrasonic scanner see your unborn child in the womb. It was also possible to have a photograph of this view. As for Grey, he wished Billy could have a sonogram every week, and he watched avidly while Billy's doctor, a handsome, rather melancholy South African named Jordan Bell, identified a series of blobs and clouds as head, shoulders, and back.

Every month in Jordan Bell's office Billy heard the sound of her own child's heart through ultrasound and what she heard sounded like galloping horses in the distance.

Billy went about her business outwardly unflapped. She continued to teach and she worked on her dissertation. In between, when she was not napping, she made lists of baby things: crib sheets, a stroller, baby T-shirts, diapers, blankets. Two months before the baby was due, she and Penny went out and bought what was needed. She was glad she had not saved this until the last minute, because in her ninth month, after an uneventful pregnancy, she was put in the hospital, where she was allowed to walk down the hall once a day. The sense of isolation she had cherished—just herself, Grey, and their unborn child—was gone. She was in the hands of nurses she had never seen before, and she found herself desperate for their companionship because she was exhausted, uncertain, and lonely in her hospital room.

Billy was admitted wearing the nice black dress Penny had made her buy and taken to a private room that overlooked the park. At the bottom of her bed were two towels and a hospital gown that tied up the back. Getting undressed to go to bed in the afternoon made her feel like a child forced to take a nap. She did not put on the hospital gown. Instead, she put on the plaid flannel nightshirt of Grey's that she had packed in her bag weeks ago in case she went into labor in the middle of the night.

"I hate it here already," Billy said.

"It's an awfully nice view," Grey said. "If it were a little further along in the season I could bring my field glasses and see what's nesting."

"I'll never get out of here," Billy said.

"Not only will you get out of here," said Grey, "you will be released a totally transformed woman. You heard Jordan—all babies get born one way or another."

If Grey was frightened, he never showed it. Billy knew that his way of dealing with anxiety was to fix his concentration, and it was now fixed on her and on being cheerful. He had never seen Billy so upset before. He held her hand.

"Don't worry," he said. "Jordan said this isn't serious. It's just a complication. The baby will be fine and you'll be fine. Besides, it won't know how to be a baby and we won't know how to be parents."

Grey had taken off his jacket and he felt a wet place where Billy had laid her cheek. He did not know how to comfort her.

"A mutual learning experience," Billy said into his arm. "I thought nature was supposed to take over and do all this for us."

"It will," Grey said.

Seven o'clock began visiting hours. Even with the door closed Billy could hear shrieks and coos and laughter. With her door open she could hear champagne corks being popped.

Grey closed the door. "You didn't eat much dinner,"

he said. "Why don't I go downstairs to the delicatessen and get you something?"

"I'm not hungry," Billy said. She did not know what was in front of her, or how long she would be in this room, or how and when the baby would be born.

"I'll call Penny and have her bring something," Grey said.

"I already talked to her," Billy said. "She and David are taking you out to dinner." David was Penny's husband, David Hooks.

"You're trying to get rid of me," Grey said.

"I'm not," Billy said. "You've been here all day, practically. I just want the comfort of knowing that you're being fed and looked after. I think you should go soon."

"It's too early," said Grey. "Fathers don't have to leave when visiting hours are over."

"You're not a father yet," Billy said. "Go."

After he left she waited by the window to watch him cross the street and wait for the bus. It was dark and cold and it had begun to sleet. When she saw him she felt pierced with desolation. He was wearing his old camel's hair coat and the wind blew through his wavy hair. He stood back on his heels as he had as a boy. He turned around and scanned the building for her window. When he saw her, he waved and smiled. Billy waved back. A taxi, thinking it was being hailed, stopped. Grey got in and was driven off.

Every three hours a nurse appeared to take her temperature, blood pressure, and pulse. After Grey had gone, the night nurse appeared. She was a tall, middle-aged black woman named Mrs. Perch. In her hand she carried what looked like a suitcase full of dials and wires.

"Don't be alarmed," Mrs. Perch said. She had a soft West Indian accent. "It is only a portable fetal heart monitor. You get to say good morning and good evening to your baby."

She squirted a blob of cold blue jelly on Billy's stomach and pushed a transducer around in it, listening for the beat. At once Billy heard the sound of galloping hooves. Mrs. Perch timed the beats against her watch.

"Nice and healthy," Mrs. Perch said.

"Which part of this baby is where?" Billy said.

"Well, his head is back here, and his back is there and here is the rump and his feet are near your ribs. Or hers, of course."

"I wondered if that was a foot kicking," Billy said.

"My second boy got his foot under my rib and kicked with all his might," Mrs. Perch said.

Billy sat up in bed. She grabbed Mrs. Perch's hand. "Is this baby going to be all right?" she said.

"Oh my, yes," Mrs. Perch said. "You're not a very interesting case. Many others much more complicated than you have done very well and you will, too."

At four in the morning, another nurse appeared, a florid Englishwoman. Billy had spent a restless night, her heart pounding, her throat dry.

"Your pressure's up, dear," said the nurse, whose tag read "M. Whitely." "Dr. Bell has written orders that if your pressure goes up you're to have a shot of hydralazine. It doesn't hurt baby—did he explain that to you?"

"Yes," said Billy groggily.

"It may give you a little headache."

"What else?"

"That's all," Miss Whitely said.

Billy fell asleep and woke with a pounding headache. When she rang the bell, the nurse who had admitted her appeared. Her name was Bonnie Near and she was Billy's day nurse. She gave Billy a pill and then taped a tongue depressor wrapped in gauze over her bed.

"What's that for?" Billy said.

"Don't ask," said Bonnie Near.

"I want to know."

Bonnie Near sat down at the end of the bed. She was a few years older than Billy, trim and wiry with short hair and tiny diamond earrings.

"It's hospital policy," she said. "The hydralazine gives you a headache, right? You ring to get something to make it go away and because you have high blood pressure everyone assumes that the blood pressure caused it, not the drug. So this thing gets taped above your bed in the one chance in about fifty-five million that you have a convulsion."

Billy turned her face away and stared out the window.

"Hey, hey," said Bonnie Near. "None of this. I noticed yesterday that you're quite a worrier. Are you like this when you're not in the hospital? Listen. I'm a straight shooter and I would tell you if I was worried about you. I'm not. You're just the common garden variety."

Every morning Grey appeared with two cups of coffee and the morning paper. He sat in a chair and he and Billy read the paper together as they did at home.

"Is the house still standing?" Billy asked after several days. "Are the banks open? Did you bring the mail? I feel I've been here ten months instead of a week."

"The mail was very boring," Grey said. "Except for this booklet from the Wisconsin Loon Society. You'll be happy to know that you can order a record called 'Loon Music.' Would you like a copy?"

"If I moved over," Billy said, "would you take off your jacket and lie down next to me?"

Grey took off his jacket and shoes, and curled up next to Billy. He pressed his nose into her face and looked as if he could drift off to sleep in a second.

"Childworld called about the crib," he said into her neck. "They want to know if we want white paint or natural pine. I said natural."

"That's what I think I ordered," Billy said. "They let the husbands stay over in this place. They call them 'dads.' "

"I'm not a dad yet, as you pointed out," Grey said. "Maybe they'll just let me take naps here."

There was a knock on the door. Grey sprang to his feet and Jordan Bell appeared.

"Don't look so nervous, Billy," he said. "I have good news. I think we want to get this baby born if your pressure isn't going to go down. I think we ought to induce you."

Billy and Grey were silent.

"The way it works is that we put you on a drip of pitocin, which is a synthetic of the chemical your brain produces when you go into labor."

"We know," Billy said. "Katherine went over it in childbirth class." Katherine Walden was Jordan Bell's nurse. "When do you want to do this?"

"Tomorrow," Jordan Bell said. "Katherine will come over and give you your last Lamaze class right here."

"And if it doesn't work?"

"It usually does," said Jordan Bell. "And if it doesn't, we do a second-day induction."

"And if that doesn't work?"

"It generally does. If it doesn't, we do a cesarean, but you'll be awake and Grey can hold your hand."

"Oh what fun," said Billy.

When Jordan Bell left, Billy burst into tears.

"Why isn't anything normal?" she said. "Why do I have to lie here day after day listening to other people's babies crying? Why is my body betraying me like this?"

Grey kissed her and then took her hands. "There is no such thing as normal," he said. "Everyone we've talked to has some story or other—huge babies that won't budge, thirty-hour labors. A cesarean is a perfectly respectable way of being born."

"What about me? What about me getting all stuck up with tubes and cut up into little pieces?" Billy said, and she was instantly ashamed. "I hate being like this. I feel I've lost myself and some whimpering, whining person has taken me over."

"Think about how in two months we'll have a two-month-old baby to take to the park."

"Do you really think everything is going to be all right?" Billy said.

"Yes," said Grey. "I do. In six months we'll be in Maine."

Billy lay in bed with her door closed reading her brochure from the Loon Society. She thought about the cottage she and Grey rented every August in Jewell Neck, Maine, on a lagoon. There at night with blackness all around them and not a light to be seen, they heard hoot owls and loons calling their night cries to one another. Loon mothers carried their chicks on their back, Billy knew. The last time she had heard those cries she had been just three months pregnant. The next time she heard them she would have a child.

She thought about the baby shower Penny had given her—a lunch party for ten women. At the end of it, Billy and Grey's unborn child had received cotton and wool blankets, little sweaters, tiny garments with feet, and two splendid Teddy bears. The Teddy bears had sat on the coffee table. Billy remembered the strange, light feeling in her chest as she looked at them. She had picked them both up and laughed with astonishment.

At a red light on the way home in a taxi, surrounded by boxes and bags of baby presents, she saw something that made her heart stop: Francis Clemens, who for two years had been Billy's illicit lover.

With the exception of her family, Billy was close only to Grey and Penny Stern. She had never been the subject of anyone's romantic passion. She and Grey, after all, had been fated to marry. She had loved him all her life.

Francis had pursued her: no one had ever pursued her before. The usual signs of romance were as unknown to Billy as the workings of a cyclotron. Crushes, she had felt, were for children. She did not really believe that adults had them.

Without her knowing it, she was incubating a number of curious romantic diseases. One day when Francis came to visit wearing his tweed coat and the ridiculously long paisley scarf he affected, she realized that she had fallen in love.

The fact of Francis was the most exotic thing that had ever happened in Billy's fairly stolid, uneventful life. He was as brilliant as a painted bunting. He was also, in marked contrast to Billy, beautifully dressed. He did not know one tree from another. He felt all birds were either robins or crows. He was avowedly urban and his pleasures were urban. He loved opera, cocktail parties, and lunches. They did not agree about economic theory, either.

Nevertheless, they spent what now seemed to Billy an enormous amount of time together. She had not sought anything like this. If her own case had been presented to her she would have dismissed it as messy, unnecessary, and somewhat sordid, but when she fell in love she fell as if backward into a swimming pool. For a while she felt dazed. Then Francis became a fact in her life. But in the end she felt her life was being ruined.

She had not seen Francis for a long time. In that brief glance at the red light she saw his paisley scarf, its long fringes flapping in the breeze. It was amazing that someone who had been so close to her did not know that she was having a baby. As the cab pulled away, she did not look back at him. She stared rigidly frontward, flanked on either side by presents for her unborn child.

The baby kicked. Mothers-to-be should not be lying in hospital beds thinking about illicit love affairs, Billy thought. Of course, if you were like the other mothers on the maternity floor and probably had never had an illicit love affair, you would not be punished by lying in the hospital in the first place. You would go into labor like everyone else, and come rushing into Maternity Admitting with your husband and your suitcase. By this time tomorrow she would have her baby in her arms, just like everyone else, but she drifted off to sleep thinking of Francis nonetheless.

* * *

At six in the morning, Bonnie Near woke her.

"You can brush your teeth," she said. "But don't drink any water. And your therapist is here to see you, but don't be long."

The door opened and Penny walked in.

"And how are we today?" she said. "Any strange dreams or odd thoughts?"

"How did you get in here?" Billy said.

"I said I was your psychiatrist and that you were being induced today and so forth," Penny said. "I just came to say good luck. Here's all the change we had in the house. Tell Grey to call constantly. I'll see you all tonight."

Billy was taken to the labor floor and hooked up to a fetal heart monitor whose transducers were kept on her stomach by a large elastic cummerbund. A stylish-looking nurse wearing hospital greens, a string of pearls, and perfectly applied pink lipstick poked her head through the door.

"Hi!" she said in a bright voice. "I'm Joanne Kelly. You're my patient today." She had the kind of voice and smile Billy could not imagine anyone's using in private. "Now, how are we? Fine? All right. Here's what we're going to do. First of all, we're going to put this IV into your arm. It will only hurt a little and then we're going to hook you up to something called pitocin. Has Dr. Bell explained any of this to you?" Joanne Kelly said.

"All," said Billy.

"Neat," Joanne Kelly said. "We *like* an informed patient. Put your arm out, please."

Billy stuck out her arm. Joanne Kelly wrapped a rubber thong under her elbow.

"Nice veins," she said. "You would have made a lovely junkie.

"Now we're going to start the pitocin," Joanne Kelly said. "We start off slow to see how you do. Then we escalate." She looked Billy up and down. "Okay," she said. "We're off and running. Now, I've got a lady huffing and puffing in the next room so I have to go and coach her. I'll be back real soon."

Billy lay looking at the clock, or watching the pitocin and glucose drip into her arm. She could not get a comfortable position and the noise of the fetal heart monitor was loud and harsh. The machine itself spat out a continual line of data.

Jordan Bell appeared at the foot of her bed.

"An exciting day—yes, Billy?" he said. "What time is Grey coming?"

"I told him to sleep late," Billy said. "All the nurses told me that this can take a long time. How am I supposed to feel when it starts working?"

"If all goes well, you'll start to have contractions and then they'll get stronger and then you'll have your baby."

"Just like that?" said Billy.

"Pretty much just like that."

But by five o'clock in the afternoon nothing much had happened.

Grey sat in a chair next to the bed. From time to time he checked the data. He had been checking it all day.

"That contraction went right off the paper," he said. "What did it feel like?"

"Intense," Billy said. "It just doesn't hurt."

"You're still in the early stages," said Jordan Bell when he came to check her. "I'm willing to stay on if you want to continue, but the baby might not be born till tomorrow."

"I'm beat," said Billy.

"Here's what we can do," Jordan said. "We can keep going or we start again tomorrow."

"Tomorrow," said Billy.

She woke up exhausted with her head pounding. The sky was cloudy and the glare hurt her eyes. She was taken to a different labor room.

In the night her blood pressure had gone up. She had begged not to have a shot—she did not see how she could go into labor feeling so terrible, but the shot was given. It had been a long, sleepless night.

She lay alone with a towel covering one eye, trying to sleep, when a nurse appeared by her side. This one looked very young, had curly hair, and thick, slightly rose-tinted glasses. Her tag read "Eva Gottlieb." Underneath she wore a button inscribed EVA: WE DELIVER.

"Hi," said Eva Gottlieb. "I'm sorry I woke you, but I'm your nurse for the day and I have to get you started."

"I'm here for a lobotomy," Billy said. "What are you going to do to me?"

"I'm going to run a line in you," Eva Gottlieb said. "And then I don't know what. Because your blood pressure is high, I'm supposed to wait until Jordan gets here." She looked at Billy carefully. "I know it's scary," she said. "But the worst that can happen is that you have to be sectioned and that's not bad."

Billy's head throbbed.

"That's easy for you to say," she said. "I'm the section."

Eva Gottlieb smiled. "I'm a terrific nurse," she said. "I'll stay with you."

Tears sprang in Billy's eyes. "Why will you?"

"Well, first of all, it's my job," said Eva. "And second of all, you look like a reasonable person."

Billy looked at Eva carefully. She felt instant, total trust. Perhaps that was part of being in hospitals and having babies. Everyone you came in contact with came very close, very fast.

Billy's eyes hurt. Eva was hooking her up to the fetal heart monitor. Her touch was strong and sure, and she seemed to know Billy did not want to be talked to. She flicked the machine on, and Billy heard the familiar sound of galloping hooves.

"Is there any way to turn it down?" Billy said.

"Sure," said Eva. "But some people find it consoling."

As the morning wore on, Billy's blood pressure continued to rise. Eva was with her constantly.

"What are they going to do to me?" Billy asked.

"I think they're probably going to give you magnesium sulfate to get your blood pressure down and then they're going to section you. Jordan does a gorgeous job, believe me. I won't let them do anything to you without explaining it first, and if you get out of bed first thing tomorrow and start moving around you'll be fine."

Twenty minutes later, a doctor Billy had never seen before administered a dose of magnesium sulfate.

"Can't you do this?" Billy asked Eva.

"It's heavy-duty stuff," Eva said. "It has to be done by a doctor."

"Can they wait until my husband gets here?"

"It's too dangerous," said Eva. "It has to be done. I'll stay with you."

The drug made her hot and flushed, and brought her

blood pressure straight down. For the next hour, Billy tried to sleep. She had never been so tired. Eva brought her cracked ice to suck on and a cloth for her head. The baby wiggled and writhed, and the fetal heart monitor gauged its every move. Finally, Grey and Jordan Bell were standing at the foot of her bed.

"Okay, Billy," said Jordan. "Today's the day. We must get the baby out. I explained to Grey about the mag sulfate. We both agree that you must have a cesarean."

"When?" Billy said.

"In the next hour," said Jordan. "I have to check two patients and then we're off to the races."

"What do you think," Billy asked Grey.

"It's right," Grey said.

"And what about you?" Billy said to Eva.

"It has to be done," Eva said.

Jordan Bell was smiling a genuine smile and he looked dashing and happy.

"Why is he so uplifted?" Billy asked Eva after he had dashed down the hall.

"He loves the OR," she said. "He loves deliveries. Think of it this way: you're going to get your baby at last."

Billy lay on a gurney, waiting to be rolled down the hall. Grey, wearing hospital scrubs, stood beside her holding her hand. She had been prepped and given an epidural anesthetic, and she could no longer feel her legs.

"Look at me," she said to Grey. "I'm a mass of tubes. I'm a miracle of modern science." She put his hand over her eyes.

Grey squatted down to put his head near hers. He

looked expectant, exhausted, and worried, but when he saw her scanning his face he smiled.

"It's going to be swell," Grey said. "We'll find out if it's little William or little Ella."

Billy's heart was pounding but she thought she ought to say something to keep her side up. She said, "I knew we never should have had sexual intercourse." Grey gripped her hand tight and smiled. Eva laughed. "Don't you guys leave me," Billy said.

Billy was wheeled down the hall by an orderly. Grey held one hand, Eva held the other. Then they left her to scrub.

She was taken to a large, pale green room. Paint was peeling on the ceiling in the corner. An enormous lamp hung over her head. The anesthetist appeared and tapped her feet.

"Can you feel this?" he said.

"It doesn't feel like feeling," Billy said. She was trying to keep her breathing steady.

"Excellent," he said.

Then Jordan appeared at her feet, and Grey stood by her head.

Eva bent down. "I know you'll hate this, but I have to tape your hands down, and I have to put this oxygen mask over your face. It comes off as soon as the baby's born, and it's good for you and the baby."

Billy took a deep breath. The room was very hot. A screen was placed over her chest.

"It's so you can't see," said Eva. "Here's the mask. I know it'll freak you out, but just breathe nice and easy. Believe me, this is going to be fast."

Billy's arms were taped, her legs were numb, and a clear plastic mask was placed over her nose and mouth. She was so frightened she wanted to cry out, but it was impossible.

Instead she breathed as Katherine Walden had taught her to. Every time a wave of panic rose, she breathed it down. Grey held her hand. His face was blank and his glasses were fogged. His hair was covered by a green cap and his brow was wet. There was nothing she could do for him, except squeeze his hand.

"Now, Billy," said Jordan Bell, "you'll feel something cold on your stomach. I'm painting you with Betadine. All right, here we go."

Billy felt something like dull tugging. She heard the sound of foamy water. Then she felt the baby being slipped from her. She turned to Grey. His glasses had unfogged and his eyes were round as quarters. She heard a high, angry scream.

"Here's your baby," said Jordan Bell. "It's a beautiful, healthy boy."

Eva lifted the mask off Billy's face.

"He's perfectly healthy," Eva said. "Listen to those lungs." She took the baby to be weighed and tested. Then she came back to Billy. "He's perfect but he's little—just under five pounds. We have to take him upstairs to the preemie nursery. It's policy when they're not five pounds."

"Give him to me," Billy said. She tried to free her hands but they were securely taped.

"I'll bring him to you," Eva said. "But he can't stay down here. He's too small. It's for the baby's safety, I promise you. Look, here he is."

The baby was held against her forehead. The moment he came near her he stopped shrieking. He was mottled and wet.

"Please let me have him," Billy said.

"He'll be fine," Eva said. They then took him away.

* * *

The next morning Billy rang for the nurse and demanded that her IV be disconnected. Twenty minutes later she was out of bed slowly walking.

"I feel as if someone had crushed my pelvic bones," Billy said.

"Someone did," said the nurse.

Two hours later she was put into a wheelchair and pushed by a nurse into the elevator and taken to the Infant Intensive Care Unit. At the door the nurse said, "I'll wheel you in."

"I can walk," Billy said. "But thank you very much."

Inside, she was instructed to scrub with surgical soap and to put on a sterile gown. Then she walked very slowly and very stiffly down the hall. A Chinese nurse stopped her.

"I'm William Delielle's mother," she said. "Where is he?"

The nurse consulted a clipboard and pointed Billy down a hallway. Another nurse in a side room pointed to an isolette—a large plastic case with porthole windows. There on a white cloth lay her child.

He was fast asleep, his little arm stretched in front of him, an exact replica of Grey's sleeping posture. On his back were two discs the size of nickels hooked up to wires that measured his temperature and his heart and respiration rates on a console above his isolette. He was long and skinny and beautiful.

"He looks like a little chicken," said Billy. "May I hold him?"

"Oh, no," said the nurse. "Not for a while. He mustn't

be stressed." She gave Billy a long look and said, "But you can open the windows and touch him."

Billy opened the porthole window and touched his leg. He shivered slightly. She wanted to disconnect his probes, scoop him up, and hold him next to her. She stood quietly, her hand resting lightly on his calf.

The room was bright, hot, and busy. Nurses came and went, washing their hands, checking charts, making notes, diapering, changing bottles of glucose solution. There were three other children in the room. One was very tiny and had a miniature IV attached to a vein in her head. A pink card was taped on her isolette. Billy looked on the side of William's isolette. There was a blue card and in Grey's tiny printing was written "William Delielle."

Later in the morning, when Grey appeared in her room he found Billy sitting next to a glass-encased pump.

"This is the well-known electric breast pump. Made in Switzerland," Billy said.

"It's like the medieval clock at Salisbury Cathedral," Grey said, peering into the glass case. "I just came from seeing William. He's much *longer* than I thought. I called all the grandparents. In fact, I was on the telephone all night after I left you." He gave her a list of messages. "They're feeding him in half an hour."

Billy looked at her watch. She had been instructed to use the pump for three minutes on each breast to begin with. Her milk, however, would not be given to William, who, the doctors said, was too little to nurse. He would be given carefully measured formula, and Billy would eventually have to wean him from the bottle and onto herself. The prospect of this seemed very remote.

As the days went by, Billy's room filled with flowers,

but she spent most of her time in the Infant ICU. She could touch William but not hold him. The morning before she was to be discharged, Billy went to William's eight o'clock feeding. She thought how lovely it would be to feed him at home, how they might sit in the rocking chair and watch the birds in the garden below. In William's present home, there was no morning and no night. He had never been in a dark room, or heard bird sounds or traffic noise, or felt a cool draft.

William was asleep on his side wearing a diaper and a little T-shirt. The sight of him seized Billy with emotion.

"You can hold him today," the nurse said.

"Yes?"

"Yes, and you can feed him today, too."

Billy bowed her head. She took a steadying breath. "How can I hold him with all this hardware on him?" she said.

"I'll show you," said the nurse. She disconnected the console, reached into the isolette, and gently untaped William's probes. Then she showed Billy how to change him, put on his T-shirt, and swaddle him in a cotton blanket. In an instant he was in Billy's arms.

He was still asleep, but he made little screeching noises and wrinkled his nose. He moved against her and nudged his head into her arm. The nurse led her to a rocking chair and for the first time she sat down with her baby.

All around her, lights blazed. The radio was on and a sweet male voice sang, "I want you to be mine, I want you to be mine, I want to take you home, I want you to be mine."

William opened his eyes and blinked. Then he yawned and began to cry.

"He's hungry," the nurse said, putting a small bottle into Billy's hand.

She fed him and burped him, and then she held him in

her arms and rocked him to sleep. In the process she fell asleep, too, and was woken by the nurse and Grey, who had come from work.

"You must put him back now," said the nurse. "He's been out a long time and we don't want to stress him."

"It's awful to think that being with his mother creates stress," Billy said.

"Oh, no!" the nurse said. "That's not what I mean. I mean, in his isolette it's temperature controlled."

Once Billy was discharged from the hospital she had to commute to see William. She went to the two morning feedings, came home for a nap, and met Grey for the five o'clock. They raced out for dinner and came back for the eight. Grey would not let Billy stay for the eleven.

Each morning she saw Dr. Edmunds, the head of neonatology. He was a tall, slow-talking, sandy-haired man with horn-rimmed glasses.

"I know you will never want to hear this under any other circumstances," he said to Billy, "but your baby is very boring."

"How boring?"

"Very boring. He's doing just what he ought to do." William had gone to the bottom of his growth curve and was beginning to gain. "As soon as he's a little fatter he's all yours."

Billy stood in front of his isolette watching William sleep.

"This is like having an affair with a married man," Billy said to the nurse who was folding diapers next to her.

The nurse looked at her uncomprehendingly.

"I mean you love the person but can only see him at certain times," said Billy.

The nurse was young and plump. "I guess I see what you mean," she said.

At home William's room was waiting. The crib had been delivered and put together by Grey. While Billy was in the hospital, Grey had finished William's room. The Teddy bears sat on the shelves. A mobile of ducks and geese hung over the crib. Grey had bought a secondhand rocking chair and had painted it red. Billy had thought she would be unable to face William's empty room. Instead she found she could scarcely stay out of it. She folded and refolded his clothes, reorganized his drawers, arranged his crib blankets. She decided what should be his homecoming clothes and set them out on the changing table along with a cotton receiving blanket and a wool shawl.

But even though he did not look at all fragile and he was beginning to gain weight, it often felt to Billy that she would never have him. She and Grey had been told ten days to two weeks from day of birth. One day when she felt she could not stand much more Billy was told that she might try nursing him.

Touch him on his cheek. He will turn to you. Guide him toward the breast and the magical connection will be made.

Billy remembered this description from her childbirth books. She had imagined a softly lit room, a sense of peacefulness, some soft, sweet music in the background.

She was put behind a screen in William's room, near an isolette containing an enormous baby who was having breathing difficulties.

She was told to keep on her sterile gown, and was given

sterile water to wash her breasts with. At the sight of his mother's naked bosom, William began to howl. The sterile gown dropped onto his face. Billy began to sweat. All around her, the nurses chatted, clattered, and dropped diapers into metal bins and slammed the tops down.

"Come on, William," Billy said. "The books say that this is the blissful union of mother and child."

But William began to scream. The nurse appeared with the formula bottle and William instantly stopped screaming and began to drink happily.

"Don't worry," the nurse said. "He'll catch on."

At night at home she sat by the window. She could not sleep. She had never felt so separated from anything in her life. Grey, to distract himself, was stenciling the wall under the molding in William's room. He had found an early American design of wheat and cornflowers. He stood on a ladder in his blue jeans carefully applying the stencil in pale blue paint.

One night Billy went to the door of the baby's room to watch him, but Grey was not on the ladder. He was sitting in the rocking chair with his head in his hands. His shoulders were shaking slightly. He had the radio on, and he did not hear her.

He had been so brave and cheerful. He had held her hand while William was born. He had told her it was like watching a magician sawing his wife in half. He had taken photos of William in his isolette and sent them to their parents and all their friends. He had read up on growth curves and had bought Billy a book on breast-feeding. He had also purloined his hospital greens to wear each year on William's birthday. Now *he* had broken down.

She made a noise coming into the room and then bent

down and stroked his hair. He smelled of soap and paint thinner. She put her arms around him, and she did not let go for a long time.

Three times a day, Billy tried to nurse William behind a screen and each time she ended up giving him his formula.

Finally she asked a nurse, "Is there some room I could sit in alone with this child?"

"We're not set up for it," the nurse said. "But I could put you in the utility closet."

There amidst used isolettes and cardboard boxes of sterile water, on the second try William nursed for the first time. She touched his cheek. He turned to her, just as it said in the book. Then her eyes crossed.

"Oh, my God!" she said.

A nurse walked in.

"Hurts, right?" she said. "Good for him. That means he's got it. It won't hurt for long."

At his evening feeding he howled again.

"The course of true love never did run smooth," said Grey. He and Billy walked slowly past the park on their way home. It was a cold, wet night.

"I am a childless mother," Billy said.

Two days later William was taken out of his isolette and put into a plastic bin. He had no temperature or heart probes, and Billy could pick him up without having to disconnect anything. At his evening feeding when the unit was quiet, she took him out in the hallway and walked up and down with him.

The next day she was greeted by Dr. Edmunds.

"I've just had a chat with your pediatrician," he said. "How would you like to take your boring baby home with you?"

"When?" said Billy.

"Right now, if you have his clothes," Dr. Edmunds said. "Dr. Jacobson will be up in a few minutes and can officially release him."

She ran down the hall and called Grey.

"Go home and get William's things," she said. "They're springing him. Come and get us."

"You mean we can just walk out of there with him?" Grey said. "I mean, just take him under our arm? He barely knows us."

"Just get here. And don't forget the blankets."

A nurse helped Billy dress William. He was wrapped in a green and white receiving blanket and covered in a white wool shawl. On his head was a blue and green knitted cap. It slipped slightly sideways, giving him a raffish look.

They were accompanied in the elevator by a nurse. It was hospital policy that a nurse hold the baby, and hand it over at the door.

It made Billy feel light-headed to be standing out of doors with her child. She felt she had just robbed a bank and got away with it.

In the taxi, Grey gave the driver their address.

"Not door to door," Billy said. "Can we get out at the avenue and walk down the street just like everyone else?"

When the taxi stopped, they got out carefully. The sky was full of silver clouds and the air was blustery and cold. William squinted at the light and wrinkled his nose.

Then, with William tight in Billy's arms, the three of them walked down the street just like everyone else.

The Augsburg Chalk Circle

Bertolt Brecht

In the days of the Thirty Years War a Swiss Protestant by the name of Zingli owned a large tannery and leather business in the free imperial city of Augsburg on the Lech. He was married to an Augsburg woman and had a child by her. As the Catholics marched on the city his friends strongly advised him to flee, but, whether it was that his small family held him back or that he did not want to abandon his tannery, he simply could not make up his mind to leave while there was yet time.

Thus he was still there when the imperial troops stormed the city and, while they plundered it that evening, he hid in a pit in the courtyard where the dyes were stored. His wife was to have moved with the child to her relatives on the outskirts, but she spent too much time packing her belongings—dresses, jewelry and bedding—and so it came about that suddenly she saw from a window on the first story a squad of imperial soldiers forcing their way into the courtyard. Beside herself with fear, she dropped everything and fled from the place through a back door.

So the child was left behind in the house. It lay in its cradle in the large hall and played with a wooden ball that hung on a string from the ceiling.

Only a young servant-girl was still in the house. She was busy with the copper pots and pans in the kitchen when she heard a noise from the street. Darting to the window she saw soldiers throwing all kinds of loot into the street from the first story of the house opposite. She ran to the hall and was just about to take the child out of the cradle when she heard the sound of heavy blows on the oaken front door. She was seized with panic and flew up the stairs.

The hall was filled with drunken soldiers, who smashed everything to pieces. They knew they were in a Protestant's house. As though by a miracle Anna, the servant-girl, remained undiscovered throughout the searching and plundering. The soldiers made off and, scrambling out of the cupboard in which she had been standing, Anna found the child in the hall, also unharmed. She snatched it up hastily and stole with it into the courtyard. In the meantime night had fallen, but the red glow from a burning house near by lit up the courtyard, and with horror she saw the battered corpse of her master. The soldiers had dragged him from his pit and butchered him.

Only now did the girl realize the danger she ran should she be caught in the street with the Protestant's child. With a heavy heart she laid it back in the cradle, gave it a little milk to drink, rocked it to sleep and made her way toward that part of the city where her married sister lived. At about ten o'clock at night, accompanied by her sister's husband, she elbowed her way through the throng of soldiers celebrating their victory to go to the outskirts and find Frau Zingli, the mother of the child. They knocked on the door of an imposing house, which, after quite a long while, did open slightly. A little old man, Frau Zingli's uncle, stuck his head out. Anna announced breathlessly that Herr Zingli was dead but the child unharmed in the house. The old man looked at her coldly with fish-like eyes and said his niece was no longer there and he himself washed his hands of the Protestant bastard. With that he shut the door again. As they left, Anna's brother-in-law noticed a curtain move at one of the windows and was convinced that Frau Zingli was there. Apparently she felt no shame in repudiating her child.

Anna and her brother-in-law walked on side by side in silence for a while. Then she declared that she wanted to go back to the tannery and fetch the child. Her brother-in-law, a quiet respectable man, listened to her aghast and tried to talk her out of this dangerous notion. What were these people to her? She had not even been decently treated.

Anna heard him out and promised to do nothing rash. Nevertheless, she must just look in quickly at the tannery to see whether the child needed anything. And she wanted to go alone.

And go she did. In the midst of the devastated hall the child lay peacefully in its cradle and slept. Wearily Anna sat down by its side and gazed at it. She had not dared to kindle a light, but the nearby house was still burning and by its light she could see the child quite well. It had a tiny mole on its little neck.

When the girl had watched the child breathing and sucking its small fist for some time, maybe an hour, she realized that she had now stayed too long and seen too much to be able to leave without the child. She got to her feet heavily and with slow movements wrapped it in its linen coverlet, picked it up in her arms and left the courtyard with it, looking round furtively like someone with a bad conscience, a thief.

After long consultations with sister and brother-in-law, she took the child to the country two weeks later, to the village of Grossaitingen, where her elder brother was a peasant. The farm belonged to his wife: he had merely married into it. It had been agreed that perhaps it would be best to tell no one but her brother who the child was, for they had never set eyes on the young wife and did not know how she would receive so dangerous a little guest.

Anna reached the village at about midday. Her brother, his wife and the farm-servants were at table. She was not ill received, but one glance at her new sister-in-law decided her to introduce the child then and there as her own. It was not until she had explained that her husband had a job at a mill in a distant village and expected her there with the child in a few weeks that the peasant woman thawed and the child was duly admired.

That afternoon she accompanied her brother to the copse to gather wood. They sat down on tree-stumps and Anna made a clean breast of it. She could see that he felt uncomfortable. His position on the farm was still insecure and he commended Anna warmly for having held her tongue in front of his wife. It was plain that he did not credit his young wife with a particularly broad-minded attitude toward the Protestant child. He wished the deception to be kept up.

However, that was not so easy as time went on.

Anna joined in the harvesting and tended "her" child

between whiles, constantly running back from the fields to the house when the others rested. The little boy thrived and even grew fat, chuckled whenever he saw Anna and made manful efforts to raise his head. But then came winter and the sister-in-law started to make inquiries about Anna's husband.

There was nothing against Anna staying on at the farm; she could make herself useful. The trouble was that the neighbors were growing curious about the father of Anna's boy, since he never came to see how he was getting on. If she could not produce a father for her child, the farm would get itself talked about before long.

One Sunday morning the peasant harnessed the horse and called Anna loudly to come with him to fetch a calf from a neighboring village. As they clattered along the road he told her that he had sought and found a husband for her. It was a dying cottager who, when the two of them stood in his mean hovel, could barely lift his wasted head from the soiled sheet.

He was willing to marry Anna. A yellow-skinned old woman, his mother, stood at the bedside. She was to have a reward for the service rendered to Anna.

The bargain was concluded in ten minutes and Anna and her brother were able to drive on and buy their calf. The wedding took place at the end of that same week. Whilst the priest mumbled the marriage ritual, the lifeless glance of the sick man did not once stray toward Anna. Her brother was in no doubt that she would have the death certificate within a few days. Then Anna's husband, the father of her child, would have died somewhere in a village near Augsburg on his way to her and no one would give the matter another thought if the widow stayed on in her brother's house.

Anna returned joyfully from her strange wedding, at

which there had been neither church bells nor a brass band, neither bridesmaids nor guests. By way of a wedding breakfast she ate a piece of bread with a slice of bacon in the larder and then, with her brother, went toward the wooden chest in which lay the child who now had a name. She tucked in the covers more tightly and smiled at her brother.

The death certificate certainly took its time.

Indeed, no word came from the old woman the next nor yet the following week. Anna had given out on the farm that her husband was at present on his way to her. When she was asked what was delaying him now she said that the deep snow must be making the journey difficult. But after another three weeks had gone by, her brother, seriously perturbed, drove to the village near Augsburg.

He came back late at night. Anna was still up and ran to the door as she heard the wheels crunch in the yard. She noticed how slowly the farmer unharnessed and a spasm went through her heart.

He brought bad tidings. On entering the hut he had found the doomed man sitting at the table in shirt-sleeves having supper, chewing away with his mouth full. He was completely restored.

The peasant did not look Anna in the face as he went on telling her. The cottager—his name, by the way, was Otterer—and his mother appeared equally astonished by the turn of events and had probably not yet decided what was to be done. Otterer had not made an unpleasant impression. He had said little, but at one point, when his mother had started lamenting that he was now saddled with an unwanted wife and a stranger's child, he had commanded her to be silent. He went on eating his cheese with deliberation throughout the interview and was still eating when the farmer took his leave.

During the following days Anna was naturally very troubled. In between her housework she taught the boy to walk. When he let go of the distaff and came tottering toward her with little outstretched arms, she suppressed a dry sob and clasped him tightly to her as she picked him up.

Once she asked her brother: "What sort of a man is he?" She had seen him only on his deathbed and then only in the evening by poor candlelight. Now she learned that her husband was a man in his fifties worn out by toil: was, in fact, what a cottager would be.

Shortly after, she saw him. With a great show of secrecy a peddler had given her a message that "a certain acquaintance" wished to meet her on such-and-such a date at such-and-such a time near such-and-such a village, at the spot where the footpath went off to Landsberg. So the married couple met midway between their villages, like the commanders of old between their battle-lines, on open ground, which was covered with snow.

Anna did not take to the man.

He had small gray teeth, looked her up and down—although she was hidden under a thick sheepskin and there was not much to be seen—and then used the words "the sacrament of marriage." She told him curtly that she would have to think things over and that he should get some dealer or slaughterer passing through Grossaitingen to tell her in her sister-in-law's hearing that he would soon be coming now and had merely been taken ill on the journey.

Otterer nodded in his deliberate way. He was more than a head taller than she and kept on glancing at the left side of her neck as they talked, which exasperated her.

But the message did not come, and Anna toyed with the idea of simply leaving the farm with the child and looking for work further south, perhaps in Kempten or Sonnthofen. Only the perils of the highway, about which there was much talk, and the fact that it was mid-winter held her back.

But now her stay at the farm grew difficult. Her sister-in-law put suspicious questions to her about her husband at the dinner table in front of all the farm-servants. When on one occasion she went so far as to glance at the child and exclaim loudly in false compassion, "poor mite!," Anna resolved to go despite everything; but at that point the child fell ill.

He lay restlessly in his wooden chest with a flushed face and clouded eyes, and Anna watched over him for nights on end with fear and hope. When he was on the road to recovery again and his smile had come back, there was a knock on the door one morning and in walked Otterer.

There was no one in the room but Anna and the child, so that she had no need to dissemble, which in any case the shock would have prevented. They stood for quite some time without a word; then Otterer announced that for his part he had thought the matter over and had come to fetch her. He referred again to the sacrament of marriage.

Anna grew angry. In a firm, though low voice she told the man she would not think of living with him, she had entered into the marriage only for the sake of the child and wanted nothing of him beyond giving her and the child his name.

As she mentioned the child Otterer glanced fleetingly toward the chest in which it lay gurgling, without, however, going up to it. This set Anna against him even more.

He voiced a few remarks: she should think things over again; there was scant fare in his home; his mother could sleep in the kitchen. Then the sister-in-law came in, greeted him inquisitively and invited him to dinner. He was already seated at table as he greeted the peasant with a careless nod, neither pretending that he did not know him nor betraying that he did. To the wife's questions he replied in monosyllables, not raising his eyes from his plate, that he had found a job in Mering and Anna could join him. But he no longer suggested that this had to be at once.

During the afternoon he avoided the brother's company and chopped wood behind the house, which no one had asked him to do. After supper, of which he again partook in silence, the sister-in-law herself carried a featherbed into Anna's room so that he could spend the night there; but at that, strange to say, he rose awkwardly to his feet and mumbled that he must get back that night. Before leaving, he gazed with an absent-minded expression into the chest where the child lay, but said nothing and did not touch him.

During the night Anna was taken ill and fell into a fever which lasted for weeks. Most of the time she lay apathetically; only now and then toward midday, when the fever abated a little, she crawled to the child's wooden chest and tucked in the covers.

In the fourth week of her illness Otterer drove into the yard in a farm cart and took her and the child away. She let this happen without a word.

Only very slowly did she regain her strength, and small wonder on the cottager's thin soup. But one morning she noticed how dirty and neglected the child looked and resolutely got up.

The little boy received her with his friendly smile in which, her brother had always declared, he took after her. He had grown and now crawled all over the room with lightning speed, slapping his hands on the floor and emitting little screams when he fell on his face. She washed him in a wooden tub and recovered her confidence.

A few days later, however, she could stand life in the hovel no longer. She wrapped the little boy in a few blankets, stuck a piece of bread and some cheese in her pocket and ran away.

She intended to reach Sonnthofen, but did not get far. She was still very weak in the knees, the highway was covered in slush and, as a result of the war, people in the villages had grown very suspicious and stingy. On the third day of her wayfaring she sprained her foot in a ditch and after many hours, during which she feared for the child, she was brought to a farmstead, where she lay in the byre. The little boy crawled about between the cows' legs and only laughed when she cried out anxiously. In the end she had to tell the farm people her husband's name and he fetched her back again to Mering.

From now on she made no further attempt to escape and accepted her lot. She worked hard. It was difficult to extract anything from the small plot and keep the tiny property going. Yet the man was not unkind to her, and the little boy ate his fill. Also her brother occasionally came over bringing a present of this or that, and once she was even able to have a little coat dyed red for the child. That, she thought, would suit a dyer's child well.

As time passed she grew quite contented and experienced many joys in bringing up the child. Thus several years went by.

But one day she went to the village to buy syrup and on her return the child was not in the hut and her husband told her that a grandly dressed lady had driven up in a coach and taken the child away. She reeled against the wall in horror, and that very evening, carrying nothing but a bundle of food, she set out for Augsburg.

Her first call in the imperial city was at the tannery. She was not admitted and could not catch sight of the child.

Her sister and brother-in-law tried in vain to console her. She ran to the authorities and, beside herself, shouted that her child had been stolen. She went so far as to hint that Protestants had stolen her child. Whereupon she learned that other times now prevailed and that peace had been concluded between Catholics and Protestants.

She would scarcely have accomplished anything had not a singular piece of luck come to her aid. Her case was referred to a judge who was a quite exceptional man.

This was the judge Ignaz Dollinger, famed throughout Swabia for his boorishness and his erudition, known to the Elector of Bavaria, whose legal dispute with the free imperial city he had had to settle, as "this Latin clodhopper," but celebrated by the people in a long ballad.

Accompanied by her sister and brother-in-law, Anna came before him. The short but immensely corpulent old man sat in a tiny bare room amidst piles of documents and listened to her only very briefly. Then he wrote something down, growled: "Step over there, and be quick about it!" and indicated with his small plump hand a spot in the room on which the light fell through a narrow window. For some minutes he studied her face closely, then waved her aside with a snort.

The next day he sent a tipstaff to fetch her and while she was still on the threshold shouted at her: "Why didn't you let on that what you're after is a tannery and the sizable property that goes with it?"

Anna said doggedly that what she was after was the child.

"Don't go thinking that you can grab the tannery," shouted the judge. "If the bastard really is yours, the property goes to Zingli's relatives."

Anna nodded without looking at him. Then she said: "He doesn't need the tannery."

"Is he yours?" barked the judge.

"Yes," she said softly. "If I could just keep him until he can say all the words. So far he only knows seven."

The judge coughed and straightened the documents on his table. Then he said more quietly, though still in an irritable tone: "You want the brat and that bitch with her five silk skirts wants him. But he needs the real mother."

"Yes," said Anna, and looked at the judge.

"Be off with you," he growled. "The Court sits on Saturday."

On that Saturday the main road and the square outside the Town Hall by the Perlach Tower were black with people who wanted to attend the proceedings over the Protestant child. This remarkable case had made a great stir from the start, and in dwellings and taverns there were arguments about who was the real and who was the false mother. Moreover, old Dollinger was renowned far and wide for his down-to-earth proceedings, his biting remarks and wise sayings. His trials drew more people than minstrels and fairs.

Thus it was not only many Augsburgers who thronged outside the Town Hall; there were also not a few farmers from the surrounding countryside. Friday was market-day and, in anticipation of the lawsuit, they had spent the night in the city.

The hall in which Judge Dollinger heard his cases was

the so-called Golden Hall. It was famous as the only hall of its size without pillars in the whole of Germany; the ceiling was suspended from the rafters by chains.

Judge Dollinger sat, a small round mountain of flesh, in front of a closed metal gate along one wall. An ordinary rope cordoned off the public. But the judge sat on the bare floor and had no table before him. He had personally instituted this setting years ago: he strongly believed in staging things properly.

Inside the roped-off enclosure were Frau Zingli with her parents, the newly arrived Swiss relatives of the late Herr Zingli—two well-dressed worthies looking like substantial merchants—and Anna Otterer with her sister. A nurse holding the child could be seen next to Frau Zingli.

Everybody, litigants and witnesses, stood. Judge Dollinger was wont to say that trials tended to be shorter if the participants had to stand. But perhaps, too, he made them stand in order to conceal himself from the public, so that people had to stand on tiptoe and crane their necks to see him.

At the start of the proceedings an incident occurred. When Anna caught sight of the child, she uttered a cry and stepped forward, and the child tried to go to her, struggled violently in the nurse's arms and started to scream. The judge ordered him to be taken out of the hall.

Then he called Frau Zingli.

She came rustling forward and described—now and again raising a little handkerchief to her eyes—how the imperial soldiers had snatched the child from her at the time of the looting. That same night the servant-girl had come to her father's place and had reported that the child was still in the house, probably in the hope of a tip. One of the father's cooks, on being sent to the tannery, had not, however, found the child, and she assumed that this person (she pointed at Anna) had taken him in order to be able to extort money in some way or other. No doubt she would have come out with such demands sooner or later had she not been deprived of the child beforehand.

Judge Dollinger called Herr Zingli's two relatives and asked them whether they had inquired after Herr Zingli at the time and what Frau Zingli had told them.

They testified that Frau Zingli had told them her husband had been killed and that she had entrusted the child to a servant-girl where it would be in good keeping. They spoke of her in a most unfriendly manner which, indeed, was no wonder, since the property would come to them if Frau Zingli lost the case.

Following their evidence the judge turned again to Frau Zingli and wanted to know from her whether she had not simply lost her head at the time of the attack and abandoned the child.

Frau Zingli looked at him with her pallid blue eyes as if in astonishment and said in injured tones that she had not abandoned her child.

Judge Dollinger cleared his throat and asked her with some interest whether she believed that no mother could abandon her child.

Yes, that was what she believed, she said firmly.

Did she then believe, the judge asked further, that a mother who nevertheless did so ought to have her behind thrashed, regardless of how many skirts she wore over it?

Frau Zingli made no answer and the judge called the former servant-girl Anna. She stepped forward quickly and said in a low voice what she had already said at the preliminary inquiry. But she talked as though she were listening at the same time, and every now and again she glanced at the big door through which the child had been taken, as though she were afraid it might still be screaming.

She testified that, although she had called at the house of Frau Zingli's uncle that night, she had not gone back to the tannery, out of fear of the imperial troops and because she was worried about her own illegitimate child which had been placed with good people in the neighboring village of Lechhausen.

Old Dollinger interrupted her rudely and snapped that at least there had been one person in the city who had felt something like fear. He was glad to be able to establish the fact, since it proved that at least one person had had some sense at the time. It was not, of course, very nice of the witness that she had only been concerned about her own child, but on the other hand, as the popular saying went, blood was thicker than water, and anyone who was a proper mother would go to the lengths of stealing for her child, though this was strictly forbidden by law, for property was property, and those who stole also lied, and lying was similarly forbidden by law. And then he gave one of his wise and pungent lectures on the infamy of people who deceived the Court till they were blue in the face; and, after a short digression on peasants who watered the milk of innocent cows and the City Council which levied too high market-taxes on the peasants—which had absolutely nothing to do with the case—he announced that the examination of witnesses was over and had led nowhere.

Then he made a long pause and showed every sign of being at a loss, gazing about him as though he expected someone or other to suggest how to arrive at a solution.

People looked at one another dumbfounded and some of them craned their necks to catch a glimpse of the helpless judge. But it remained very quiet in the hall; only the crowd in the street below could be heard.

Then, sighing, the judge began to speak again.

"It has not been established who is the real mother," he said. "The child is to be pitied. We have all heard of fathers dodging their duty and not wanting to be fathers—the rogues!—but here are two mothers both laying claim. The Court has listened to them as long as they deserve, namely a full five minutes to each, and the Court is convinced that both are lying like a book. But, as already said, we still have to think of the child who must have a mother. Therefore it has to be established, without paying attention to mere babble, who the real mother of the child is."

And in a cross voice he called the usher and ordered him to bring a piece of chalk.

The usher went and fetched a piece of chalk.

"Draw a circle with the chalk on the floor big enough for three people to stand in," the judge directed him.

The usher knelt down and drew the circle with the chalk as requested.

"Now fetch the child," ordered the judge.

The child was brought in. He started to howl again and tried to go to Anna. Old Dollinger took no notice of the crying and merely delivered his address in a rather louder voice.

"This test which is now about to be applied," he announced, "I found in an old book and it is considered extremely good. The simple idea underlying the test with the chalk circle is that the real mother will be recognized by her love for the child. Hence the strength of this love must be tested. Usher, place the child in that chalk circle."

The usher took the wailing child from the nurse's hand and led him into the circle. The judge went on, turning toward Frau Zingli and Anna:

"You go and stand in the chalk circle too; each of you take one of the child's hands and when I say 'go!' try and pull the child out of the circle. Whichever of you has the stronger love will also pull with the greater strength and thus bring the child to her side."

There was a stir in the hall. The spectators stood on tiptoe and had words with those standing in front of them.

But there was dead silence again as the two women stepped into the circle and each grasped one of the child's hands. The child had also fallen silent, as though he sensed what was at stake. He turned his little tear-stained face up to Anna. Then the judge gave the order "Go!"

And with a single violent jerk Frau Zingli tore the child out of the chalk circle. Bewildered and incredulous, Anna's eyes followed him. For fear that he might come to harm if both his little arms were pulled in two directions at once, she had immediately let go.

Old Dollinger stood up.

"And thus we know," he said loudly, "who is the right mother. Take the child away from the slut. She would tear him to pieces in cold blood."

And he nodded to Anna and quickly left the hall to have his breakfast.

And in the following weeks the peasants round about, who were pretty wide-awake, talked of how the judge on awarding the child to the woman from Mering had winked at her.

Mothers and Daughters

Jane Goodall

"Manners makyth man," wrote the poet William of Wykeham. Ah—but what makyth the manners? We might, perhaps, venture "Mother makyth manners"—along, of course, with a dash of early experience and more than a little spicing of genetic inheritance. The relative roles of "nature" versus "nurture" caused much bitter argument in scientific circles in recent years. But the flames of the controversy have now died down, and it is generally accepted that, even in the lower animals, adult behavior is acquired through a mix of genetic make-up and experience gained as the individual goes through life. The more complex an animal's brain the greater the role that learning is likely to play in shaping its behavior, and the more variation we shall find between one individual and another. Information acquired and lessons learned during infancy and childhood, when behavior is at its most flexible, are likely to have particular significance.

For chimpanzees, whose brains are more like those of humans than are those of any other living animal, the nature of early experience may have a profound effect on adult behavior. Particularly important, I believe, is the disposition of the child's mother, his or her position in the family, and, if there are elder siblings, their sex and personalities. A secure childhood is likely to lead to self-reliance and independence in adulthood. A disturbed early life may leave permanent scars. In the wild almost all mothers look after their infants relatively efficiently. But even so there are clear-cut differences in the child-raising techniques of different individuals. It would be hard to find two females whose mothers had treated them more differently during their early years, than Flo's daughter Fifi and Passion's daughter Pom. In fact, Flo and Passion are at opposite ends of a scale: most mothers fall somewhere between these two extremes.

Fifi had a carefree—a wonderful—childhood. Old Flo was a highly competent mother, affectionate, tolerant, playful and protective. Figan was an integral part of the family when Fifi was growing up, joining her games when Flo was not in the mood and often supporting his young sister in her childhood squabbles. Faben, Flo's oldest son, was often around too. Flo, who held top rank among the females when I first knew her, was a sociable female. She spent a good deal of time with other members of her community, and she had a relaxed and friendly relationship with most of the adult males. In this social environment Fifi became a self-confident and assertive child.

Pom's childhood, in comparison with Fifi's, was bleak. Passion's personality was as different from Flo's as chalk from cheese. Even when I first knew her in the early sixties she was a loner. She had no close female companions, and on those occasions when she was in a group with adult males her relationship with them was typically uneasy and tense. She was a cold mother, intolerant and brusque, and she seldom played with her infant, particularly during the first two years. And Pom, being the first surviving child, had no sibling to play with during the long hours when she and her mother were on their own. She had a difficult time during her early months, and she became an anxious and clinging child, always fearful that her mother would go off and leave her behind.

Thus it is not really surprising that Pom and Fifi reacted differently to the various challenges that a young female must face as she grows up in the wild.

All chimpanzee infants become upset and depressed during the difficult time of weaning when the mother prevents her child, with increasing frequency and determination, both from suckling and from riding on her back. This usually takes place during the fourth year. Fifi became noticeably less cheerful and less playful for a few months and she spent more and more time sitting in close contact with her mother, looking hunched and sad. But she got over her depression quickly, and by the time her infant brother Flint was born, was back to her old self—outgoing, confident and assertive.

Pom's depression, however, seemed to go on forever. Interestingly, sometime during her daughter's third year, Passion's attitude toward her had softened: she had become more patient and more playful. And Pom, presumably as a direct result of this, had gradually become less anxious. But these signs of improved psychological well-being disappeared during the trauma of weaning. It was clearly a far more disturbing experience for Pom than it had been for Fifi, despite the fact that Passion, to my surprise, was remarkably tolerant. She almost always responded to Pom's frequent requests for grooming and even allowed her to ride on her back with a minimum of protest. For weeks after we were sure that her milk had dried up, she let Pom sit close, a nipple in her mouth, her eyes often closed, for as long as twenty minutes at a time. But nothing seemed to help. Pom's inability to cope with weaning was almost certainly due to the harsh treatment she had received as an infant. So often her only succor had been her mother's milk and now, when this was suddenly denied, her early sense of insecurity returned. It was not until a few weeks before Passion gave birth to her next infant that Pom finally quit trying to suckle from her mother.

For all young chimps the birth of a new baby in the family signals the end of an era, a major step toward independence—although it will be another three to six years before they begin to leave their mothers and move out into the adult world. Fifi was about five and a half years old when Flint was born. Now that Flo had a tiny infant to care for she could not give her undivided attention to Fifi. But far from being upset, Fifi was utterly fascinated and delighted by the new baby, and spent hours, during his first two years, playing with him, grooming him, and carrying him during family travel. She jealously chased off other youngsters when they wanted to play with him, at least when he was small, and helped Flo by retrieving him from potentially dangerous situations.

Pom, like Fifi, was initially curious and fascinated when infant Prof was born. But soon, after the novelty of her little brother had worn off, she reverted to the depressed state in which she had been before his birth. And she remained lethargic and listless for most of Prof's first year of life, seldom showing much interest in him. Even when, at five months old, he began to toddle about—a stage that Fifi had found irresistible—Pom remained unresponsive to Prof. She seldom carried him, and when they played, which was not often, the game was usually initiated by Prof. Gradually, however, Pom got over her depression, and her brother then became more appealing. She began to carry him and play with him more often. She became very protective, too. Once, for example, as Pom led her family through the forest, she noticed a large snake coiled up beside the trail. Uttering a small warning "huu," she swung up into a tree. Three-year-old Prof, tottering along behind his sister, seemed not to see the snake. If he did, he had no thought of possible danger. Nor, apparently, did he understand Pom's soft warning. Passion, bringing up the rear, was far behind. Suddenly, when Prof was within a few yards of the snake, Pom, every hair on end with fright, rushed down, gathered up her little brother, and climbed with him to safety.

The next major upheaval in the life of a young female chimpanzee is when, at about ten years of age, she becomes for the first time sexually attractive to the big males. Fifi was enchanted by this new experience. Sometimes, when a male was, quite obviously, uninterested in what she had to offer, she would recline close by and, ever hopeful, stare at him. Or rather, stare at a certain portion of his anatomy that was, so far as she was concerned, disappointingly flabby. Once she went so far as to tweak the limp appendage—with highly satisfactory results! It soon became clear that the males regarded Fifi as a most desirable sexual partner. She did not have quite the sex appeal that Flo had once radiated—but in those days she was, after all, younger and less experienced.

When Pom, in her turn, first became sexually attractive to the adult males she, like Fifi, clearly found the new experience pleasurable and hastened to any male who showed signs of interest. But whereas Fifi had been calm and relaxed when she complied with the sexual demands of the males, Pom crouched before them, tense and nervous, and the moment intercourse was over she leapt away, often screaming. She developed strange, neurotic behaviors. Often, for example, as she went up to a male to greet him, she would utter loud and frenzied pant-barks of submission and, crouching in front of him, dab a hand out toward his face, then leap away. The males were irritated by this and sometimes threatened or even attacked her. And so, in a vicious circle, her nervousness and tension increased. It was scarcely surprising that Pom was far less popular as a sexual partner than Fifi had been at the same age.

Adolescent female chimpanzees, like their human counterparts, typically go through an infertile phase between menarche and the first conception. For both Fifi and Pom this period lasted for about two years—two years during which, for about ten days each month, they came into estrus and were sexually attractive and highly receptive to the adult males. These months were clearly beneficial to Fifi. Although Flo sometimes accompanied her daughter when she went in search of male company, she was old, and Fifi often went without her. And so she learned how to get on in adult society without having to rely on support from her high-ranking mother. As she matured socially and became more self-reliant, she filled out and became stronger too—she would be the more able to cope when she eventually became a mother herself.

Nevertheless, while Fifi became increasingly independent and worldly-wise, she always rejoined her mother after each period of dalliance with the males. And so she was still very much a part of the family when, in 1968, Flo gave birth to her last baby. Sadly, little Flame only lived for six months, but during that time Fifi, whenever she had the opportunity—when she was not sexually preoccupied with the males—delighted to carry, groom and gently play with the tiny infant, thus gaining additional experience in maternal skills.

Toward the end of her two-year period of infertility, Fifi was frequently taken off by one or other of her male suitors to the outskirts of the community range. There the couple would remain—if the male could pull it off—isolated from other males, for the duration of Fifi's swelling. It is during such consortships that males have a good chance of siring a child. In fact, though, it is fairly certain that Fifi's first infant was not fathered by a male of her own community, but by one of the Kalande males in the south—for Fifi made a number of visits to their territory, obeying the peculiar urge to wander, to meet and mate with stranger males, that we have observed in most females during late adolescence. And it seems that she conceived during one of those excursions. Once pregnant, Fifi returned to her own home range. Her relationship with Flo and seven-year-old Flint became even closer now that her sexual urge was, for a while, quiescent.

Pom's adolescence was more turbulent. By then the bond between herself and her mother was very close indeed—even closer, in some ways, than that between Fifi and Flo.

Passion would always back up her daughter during squabbles with other community females and Pom had become assertive and aggressive in her dealings with them. When Passion was not close by, the others would often retaliate, picking a fight with Pom. But if Passion was close enough to hear her daughter's screaming she would race to her defense and mother and daughter together would then punish the female concerned. And Pom typically tried to help and support her mother in the same way.

One such incident is clear in my mind. I had followed Pom all morning and was watching as she and another female, Nope, fished for termites. Presently we heard pant-hoots, then some screams, about half a mile to the west, further down the valley. Both females stared toward the sounds but while Nope at once returned to her feeding, Pom continued to gaze westward. After a few moments there was another outburst of calling. Nope paid no attention, but Pom gave a little grin of fear, reached to touch Nope, and continued to look toward the distant group. A minute later came the frenzied screaming of a chimpanzee being attacked. Instantly, with a squeak of fear, Pom was off, racing toward the sounds. There was, fortunately for me, a rough trail and I was not left too far behind. We ran for about five hundred yards and then, as I burst through a tangle of vines, I saw that Pom had joined her mother and was grooming her. Both Passion and Prof, who was up in a tree above, were bleeding from fresh wounds, received, without doubt, during the attacks we had just heard. An adult male charged toward us, hit out at Passion and her daughter, then charged away, leaving the family alone.

Even during the periods when Pom was pink and went off in search of sexual gratification, Passion often went with her. And if Pom did travel with the males on her own, she usually returned quite soon to the reassuring company of her mother and little Prof. Not until her sixth pinkness was Pom observed to sleep with a group of males far away from her family.

Unlike Fifi, Pom was seldom taken on consortships—and at least part of the reason lay in her unusually close relationship with Passion. I well remember one hot September afternoon in 1976, when at midday I found Pom accompanied, as usual, by her mother and brother. With them was Satan—and he was trying most desperately to lead Pom away to the north. Pom, however, had no desire to go with him. Again and again, hair bristling, eyes glaring, Satan swayed vegetation at the young female, then moved off in his chosen direction, looking back to see if she was following. Again and again Pom ignored these summonses. Several times, exasperated, Satan swaggered around Pom, threatening her. And when this happened Pom, screaming loudly, rushed to Passion for comfort. Then Passion, tough old bird that she was, glared at the big male and uttered a string of angry—and surely abusive—waa-barks. Once Satan attacked Pom, and immediately Passion, with furious barks, hurled herself at her daughter's assailant, hitting him with her fists. Satan was probably as surprised as I was! He left the daughter and turned on the mother—but he only attacked her mildly. Passion and Pom then groomed each other for a long time while Satan sat, glowering, nearby. After this he made only two more swaggering attempts to impose his will—and then, nearly four hours after I had first encountered them, he gave up and went off on his own. Pom had been well chaperoned!

The birth of a first baby, is, for the mother, an event of epic significance. And in Fifi's case the birth was of great significance for me also. Indeed, during the eight months of

Fifi's pregnancy I was almost (but not quite!) as impatient as I had been during my own pregnancy four years earlier. Would she, as I predicted, be the same kind of mother as Flo? We first saw her baby in May 1971 when he was about two days old. Remembering the wild sexual adventures of his mother's adolescence, we named him—naturally enough—Freud! Just as expected, Fifi was from the start a relaxed and competent mother. Like Flo before her, she was tolerant, affectionate and playful. And she too showed some of the behavior that had been unique to her mother.

One day, when Freud was just a few months old, a student called to me: "Isn't that what Flo used to do?" And there was Fifi dangling Freud from one foot while she tickled him just as Flo had played with Flint! Until then, no other mother had been observed to play in that special way. Fifi had tried when, as a child, she played with little Flint, but in those days her legs had been too short. Now she imitated Flo to perfection.

Fifi continued to spend most of her time with her own mother during Freud's first year of life, but disappointingly, Flo showed little interest in her grandson. Sometimes she peered at him and, as he grew older, she tolerated him when he occasionally held onto her hair. But by then Flo was very old indeed; she had barely enough energy to get her frail body through each day and there was none left over for luxuries such as playing with her daughter's infant. Freud was only fifteen months old when his grandmother died.

And what of Pom and her first baby? She was almost exactly thirteen years old when Pan was born. I had expected her to treat him much as she herself had been treated as an infant but in this case (fortunately for Pan) my predictions were largely wrong. Pom was most definitely a more attentive and tolerant mother than Passion had been. Indeed, when first I watched her with her baby, carefully supporting him during travel whenever he lost his grip, it seemed that she had the makings of a really considerate mother. But there was something lacking: Pom did not develop anything like the degree of maternal proficiency and concern shown by Fifi.

Indeed, in some ways Pom's behavior did reflect the manner in which she herself had been handled as an infant. She found it difficult to cradle Pan comfortably when he was small—or else she simply couldn't be bothered. Often, as she sat in a tree, the infant would slip down off her lap and hang on frantically with wildly kicking legs as he tried to pull himself back up again. Only when he whimpered did Pom look down and, appearing slightly surprised, gather him back onto her thighs. But she seldom made any attempt to make a better lap and often, after a few minutes, he slipped down again and the sequence was repeated. Pom, like Passion, tended to move off without first gathering her infant; but unlike Passion, Pom almost always hurried back at his first whimper of distress. It seemed that she always expected Pan would be able to follow, but was instantly concerned when she found that he could not. Pom, like Passion, was not a playful mother, but Pan did not suffer as a result since Pom continued to spend most of her time with Passion and her new infant, Pax. And Pax, just a year older than Pan, was the perfect playmate.

Pom, for all that she was a far better mother than I had expected, lost this first child. I was there to witness the horrifying accident that led to his death. It was one of those violently blustery mornings in August when the wind roars down the valley in great gusts, tossing the tree tops and sweeping on to wreak havoc over the lake. For about half an hour I had been lying on my back watching Pom and Pan as they fed on oil nuts forty-five feet above me. Pan was almost three years old, able to poke the occasional fruit from its horny case though preferring to beg for a half-chewed one from his mother. For a while he clung tightly to Pom's hair, made nervous, as most chimps are, by the violent wind. But then he got bold and ventured further afield despite the gale. Suddenly a really fierce gust lashed savagely at the fronds and Pan, like a stuffed toy, was swept from the tree. He seemed almost to float through the air, his arms and legs spread-eagled, as though he was lying flat out on some buoyant but invisible air mattress. As he hit the ground, rock hard after the fierce suns of summer, there was a sickening thud. A moment later came two strangled, heart-wrenching exhalations, then silence.

I was shaking when I moved toward his body. He lay as he had fallen, on his back. His eyes were closed. I looked up at Pom, left alone so suddenly in the tree. She was staring down at the ground. Very slowly, as though afraid, she climbed down and approached her infant. Cautiously she reached out, and gathered up the tiny form. To my utter astonishment he gripped her hair and clung, unaided, as she moved away. I had been certain he was already dead.

For the next two hours Pom rested and groomed her infant. No mother could have shown more concern, more solicitude. Pan suckled for a long time, then leaned against Pom, with his eyes closed. When he did move, it was very slowly and, not surprisingly, he seemed quite dazed. I assumed he was, at the very least, suffering from concussion. Presently Pom gathered up her battered child and carried him up into a tall tree to feed.

Unfortunately this happened the day I was due to leave Gombe. The boat was waiting and I could not follow the tragedy through to the end. Three days later, when Pom was next seen, Pan was dead. Presumably he sustained internal injuries or a fractured skull—or both. By a strange coincidence, three weeks later, in Dar es Salaam, a little boy, the seven-year-old son of my neighbor's cook, fell from a coconut palm and landed, like Pan, on his back. He was rushed to the hospital where they found extensive internal damage, including a ruptured liver. They patched him up as best they could, but he too died a short while afterwards.

It would be unfair to blame Pom entirely for the accident, to accuse her of negligence. It could have happened to any infant. Yet I cannot imagine Fifi losing a child in this way. For Fifi, like Flo before her, like all really attentive chimpanzee mothers, is alert to potential danger. Often she "rescues" her infant before the child itself has shown any sign of distress or fear. After Pan's death, I began to watch carefully whenever Fifi, with one of her infants, fed up in a palm tree during a strong wind. Always the infant stayed close to her. Although I could not determine whether that was due to Fifi's concern or the apprehension of the child, in some ways it comes to the same thing: if the infant is extra cautious it is probably at least in part because its movements have been firmly restricted in similar circumstances in the past.

Pom, after the tragic death of little Pan, became sick, lethargic and so emaciated we thought she might not recover. Her relationship with her mother now became, if anything, even closer, and they were seldom apart. I remember one day when they did accidentally become separated. Pom searched for Passion for almost an hour, frequently whimpering softly to herself, and from time to time climbing tall trees and gazing out from these vantage points in all directions. To some extent she may have been helped by occasional whiffs of Passion's characteristic odor for, as she traveled, she repeatedly bent and sniffed the trail or picked up leaves and smelled them carefully before dropping them. When eventually mother and daughter were reunited, Pom rushed up to Passion with small squeaks of excitement and pleasure, and the two groomed for over an hour.

As we shall see, the life histories of Fifi and Pom have continued along very different lines. Pom, after her mother's death, became increasingly solitary and eventually left the community for good. Fifi, by contrast, has become one of the most high-ranking and respected females in her group, maintaining close friendly relations with the adult males and many females too. She has also become the most reproductively successful Kasakela female to date. Whether Flo's main contribution to Fifi was genetic or through child-raising skills or through the equal mix of the two, the recipe worked. And her two eldest sons, who also received fifty percent of their genes from their mother and who were probably brought up in much the same way, thrived on Flo's recipe too. Particularly the younger of the two, Figan, who became, for a while, the most powerful alpha male in Gombe's recorded history.

My Oedipus Complex

Frank O'Connor

Father was in the army all through the war—the first war, I mean—so, up to the age of five, I never saw much of him, and what I saw did not worry me. Sometimes I woke and there was a big figure in khaki peering down at me in the candlelight. Sometimes in the early morning I heard the slamming of the front door and the clatter of nailed boots down the cobbles of the lane. These were Father's entrances and exits. Like Santa Claus he came and went mysteriously.

In fact, I rather liked his visits, though it was an uncomfortable squeeze between Mother and him when I got into the big bed in the early morning. He smoked, which gave him a pleasant musty smell, and shaved, an operation of astounding interest. Each time he left a trail of souvenirs—model tanks and Gurkha knives with handles made of bullet cases, and German helmets and cap badges and button-sticks, and all sorts of military equipment—carefully stowed away in a long box on top of the wardrobe, in case they ever came in handy. There was a bit of the magpie about Father; he expected everything to come in handy. When his back was turned, Mother let me get a chair and rummage through his treasures. She didn't seem to think so highly of them as he did.

The war was the most peaceful period of my life. The window of my attic faced southeast. My mother had curtained it, but that had small effect. I always woke with the first light and, with all the responsibilities of the previous day melted, feeling myself rather like the sun, ready to illumine and rejoice. Life never seemed so simple and clear and full of possibilities as then. I put my feet out from under the clothes—I called them Mrs. Left and Mrs. Right—and invented dramatic situations for them in which they discussed the problems of the day. At least Mrs. Right did; she was very demonstrative, but I hadn't the same control of Mrs. Left, so she mostly contented herself with nodding agreement.

They discussed what Mother and I should do during the day, what Santa Claus should give a fellow for Christmas, and what steps should be taken to brighten the home. There was that little matter of the baby, for instance. Mother and I could never agree about that. Ours was the only house in the terrace without a new baby, and Mother said we couldn't afford one till Father came back from the war because they cost seventeen and six. That showed how simple she was. The Geneys up the road had a baby, and everyone knew they couldn't afford seventeen and six. It was probably a cheap baby, and Mother wanted something really good, but I felt she was too exclusive. The Geneys' baby would have done us fine.

Having settled my plans for the day, I got up, put a chair under the attic window, and lifted the frame high enough to stick out my head. The window overlooked the front gardens of the terrace behind ours, and beyond these it looked over a deep valley to the tall, red-brick houses terraced up the opposite hillside, which were all still in shadow, while those at our side of the valley were all lit up, though with long strange shadows that made them seem unfamiliar; rigid and painted.

After that I went into Mother's room and climbed into the big bed. She woke and I began to tell her of my schemes. By this time, though I never seem to have noticed it, I was petrified in my nightshirt, and I thawed as I talked until, the last frost melted, I fell asleep beside her and woke again only when I heard her below in the kitchen, making the breakfast.

After breakfast we went into town; heard Mass at St. Augustine's and said a prayer for Father, and did the shopping. If the afternoon was fine we either went for a walk in the country or a visit to Mother's great friend in the convent, Mother St. Dominic. Mother had them all praying for Father, and every night, going to bed, I asked God to send him back safe from the war to us. Little, indeed, did I know what I was praying for!

One morning, I got into the big bed, and there, sure enough, was Father in his usual Santa Claus manner, but later, instead of uniform, he put on his best blue suit, and Mother was as pleased as anything. I saw nothing to be pleased about, because, out of uniform, Father was altogether less interesting, but she only beamed, and explained that our prayers had been answered, and off we went to Mass to thank God for having brought Father safely home.

The irony of it! That very day when he came in to dinner he took off his boots and put on his slippers, donned the dirty old cap he wore about the house to save him from colds, crossed his legs, and began to talk gravely to Mother, who looked anxious. Naturally, I disliked her looking anxious, because it destroyed her good looks, so I interrupted him.

"Just a moment, Larry!" she said gently.

This was only what she said when we had boring visitors, so I attached no importance to it and went on talking.

"Do be quiet, Larry!" she said impatiently. "Don't you hear me talking to Daddy?"

This was the first time I had heard those ominous words, "talking to Daddy," and I couldn't help feeling that if this was how God answered prayers, he couldn't listen to them very attentively.

"Why are you talking to Daddy?" I asked with as great a show of indifference as I could muster.

"Because Daddy and I have business to discuss. Now, don't interrupt again!"

In the afternoon, at Mother's request, Father took me for a walk. This time we went into town instead of out the country, and I thought at first, in my usual optimistic way, that it might be an improvement. It was nothing of the sort. Father and I had quite different notions of a walk in town. He had no proper interest in trams, ships, and horses, and the only thing that seemed to divert him was talking to fellows as old as himself. When I wanted to stop he simply went on, dragging me behind him by the hand; when he wanted to stop I had no alternative but to do the same. I noticed that it seemed to be a sign that he wanted to stop for a long time whenever he leaned against a wall. The second time I saw him do it I got wild. He seemed to be settling himself forever. I pulled him by the coat and trousers, but, unlike Mother who, if you were too persistent, got into a wax and said: "Larry, if you don't behave yourself, I'll give you a good slap," Father had an extraordinary capacity for amiable inattention. I sized him up and wondered would I cry, but he seemed to be too remote to be annoyed even by that. Really, it was like going for a walk with a mountain! He either ignored the wrenching and pummeling entirely, or else glanced down with a grin of amusement from his peak. I had never met anyone so absorbed in himself as he seemed.

At teatime, "talking to Daddy" began again, complicated this time by the fact that he had an evening paper, and every few minutes he put it down and told Mother something new out of it. I felt this was foul play. Man for man, I was prepared to compete with him any time for Mother's attention, but when he had it all made up for him by other people it left me no chance. Several times I tried to change the subject without success.

"You must be quiet while Daddy is reading, Larry," Mother said impatiently.

It was clear that she either genuinely liked talking to Father better than talking to me, or else that he had some terrible hold on her which made her afraid to admit the truth.

"Mummy," I said that night when she was tucking me up, "do you think if I prayed hard God would send Daddy back to the war?"

She seemed to think about that for a moment.

"No, dear," she said with a smile. "I don't think he would."

"Why wouldn't he, Mummy?"

"Because there isn't a war any longer, dear."

"But, Mummy, couldn't God make another war, if He liked?"

"He wouldn't like to, dear. It's not God who makes wars, but bad people."

"Oh!" I said.

I was disappointed about that. I began to think that God wasn't quite what he was cracked up to be.

Next morning I woke at my usual hour, feeling like a bottle of champagne. I put out my feet and invented a long conversation in which Mrs. Right talked of the trouble she had with her own father till she put him in the Home. I didn't quite know what the Home was but it sounded the right place for Father. Then I got my chair and stuck my head out of the attic window. Dawn was just breaking, with a guilty air that made me feel I had caught it in the act. My head bursting with stories and schemes, I stumbled in next door, and in the half-darkness scrambled into the big bed. There was no room at Mother's side so I had to get between her and Father. For the time being I had forgotten about him, and for several minutes I sat bolt upright, racking my brains to know what I could do with him. He was taking up more than his fair share of the bed, and I couldn't get comfortable, so I gave him several kicks that made him grunt and stretch. He made room all right, though. Mother waked and felt for me. I settled back comfortably in the warmth of the bed with my thumb in my mouth.

"Mummy!" I hummed, loudly and contentedly.

"Sssh! dear," she whispered. "Don't wake Daddy!"

This was a new development, which threatened to be even more serious than "talking to Daddy." Life without my early-morning conferences was unthinkable.

"Why?" I asked severely.

"Because poor Daddy is tired."

This seemed to me a quite inadequate reason, and I was sickened by the sentimentality of her "poor Daddy." I never liked that sort of gush; it always struck me as insincere.

"Oh!" I said lightly. Then in my most winning tone: "Do you know where I want to go with you today, Mummy?"

"No, dear," she sighed.

"I want to go down the Glen and fish for thornybacks with my new net, and then I want to go out to the Fox and Hounds, and—"

"Don't-wake-Daddy!" she hissed angrily, clapping her hand across my mouth.

But it was too late. He was awake, or nearly so. He grunted and reached for the matches. Then he stared incredulously at his watch.

"Like a cup of tea, dear?" asked Mother in a meek, hushed voice I had never heard her use before. It sounded almost as though she were afraid.

"Tea?" he exclaimed indignantly. "Do you know what the time is?"

"And after that I want to go up the Rathcooney Road," I said loudly, afraid I'd forget something in all those interruptions.

"Go to sleep at once, Larry!" she said sharply.

I began to snivel. I couldn't concentrate, the way that pair went on, and smothering my early-morning schemes was like burying a family from the cradle.

Father said nothing, but lit his pipe and sucked it, looking out into the shadows without minding Mother or me. I knew he was mad. Every time I made a remark Mother hushed me irritably. I was mortified. I felt it wasn't fair; there was even something sinister in it. Every time I had pointed out to her the waste of making two beds when we could both sleep in one, she had told me it was healthier like that, and now here was this man, this stranger, sleeping with her without the least regard for her health!

He got up early and made tea, but though he brought Mother a cup he brought none for me.

"Mummy," I shouted, "I want a cup of tea, too."

"Yes, dear," she said patiently. "You can drink from Mummy's saucer."

That settled it. Either Father or I would have to leave the house. I didn't want to drink from Mother's saucer; I wanted to be treated as an equal in my own home, so, just to spite her, I drank it all and left none for her. She took that quietly, too.

But that night when she was putting me to bed she said gently:

"Larry, I want you to promise me something."

"What is it?" I asked.

"Not to come in and disturb poor Daddy in the morning. Promise?"

"Poor Daddy" again! I was becoming suspicious of everything involving that quite impossible man.

"Why?" I asked.

"Because poor Daddy is worried and tired and he doesn't sleep well."

"Why doesn't he, Mummy?"

"Well, you know, don't you, that while he was at the war Mummy got the pennies from the Post Office?"

"From Miss MacCarthy?"

"That's right. But now, you see, Miss MacCarthy

hasn't any more pennies, so Daddy must go out and find us some. You know what would happen if he couldn't?"

"No," I said, "tell us."

"Well, I think we might have to go out and beg for them like the poor old woman on Fridays. We wouldn't like that, would we?"

"No," I agreed. "We wouldn't."

"So you'll promise not to come in and wake him?"

"Promise."

Mind you, I meant that. I knew pennies were a serious matter, and I was all against having to go out and beg like the old woman on Fridays. Mother laid out all my toys in a complete ring round the bed so that, whatever way I got out, I was bound to fall over one of them.

When I woke I remembered my promise all right. I got up and sat on the floor and played—for hours, it seemed to me. Then I got my chair and looked out the attic window for more hours. I wished it was time for Father to wake; I wished someone would make me a cup of tea. I didn't feel in the least like the sun; instead, I was bored and so very, very cold! I simply longed for the warmth and depth of the big featherbed.

At last I could stand it no longer. I went into the next room. As there was still no room at Mother's side I climbed over her and she woke with a start.

"Larry," she whispered, gripping my arm very tightly, "what did you promise?"

"But I did, Mummy," I wailed, caught in the very act. "I was quiet for ever so long."

"Oh, dear, and you're perished!" she said sadly, feeling me all over. "Now, if I let you stay will you promise not to talk?"

"But I want to talk, Mummy," I wailed.

"That has nothing to do with it," she said with a firmness that was new to me. "Daddy wants to sleep. Now, do you understand that?"

I understood it only too well. I wanted to talk, he wanted to sleep—whose house was it, anyway?

"Mummy," I said with equal firmness, "I think it would be healthier for Daddy to sleep in his own bed."

That seemed to stagger her, because she said nothing for a while.

"Now, once for all," she went on, "you're to be perfectly quiet or go back to your own bed. Which is it to be?"

The injustice of it got me down. I had convicted her out of her own mouth of inconsistency and unreasonableness, and she hadn't even attempted to reply. Full of spite, I gave Father a kick, which she didn't notice but which made him grunt and open his eyes in alarm.

"What time is it?" he asked in a panic-stricken voice, not looking at Mother but at the door, as if he saw someone there.

"It's early yet," she replied soothingly. "It's only the child. Go to sleep again . . . Now, Larry," she added, getting out of bed, "you've wakened Daddy and you must go back."

This time, for all her quiet air, I knew she meant it, and knew that my principal rights and privileges were as good as lost unless I asserted them at once. As she lifted me, I gave a screech, enough to wake the dead, not to mind Father. He groaned.

"That damn child! Doesn't he ever sleep?"

"It's only a habit, dear," she said quietly, though I could see she was vexed.

"Well, it's time he got out of it," shouted Father, beginning to heave in the bed. He suddenly gathered all the bedclothes about him, turned to the wall, and then looked back over his shoulder with nothing showing only two small, spiteful, dark eyes. The man looked very wicked.

To open the bedroom door, Mother had to let me down, and I broke free and dashed for the farthest corner, screeching. Father sat bolt upright in bed.

"Shut up, you little puppy!" he said in a choking voice.

I was so astonished that I stopped screeching. Never, never had anyone spoken to me in that tone before. I looked at him incredulously and saw his face convulsed with rage. It was only then that I fully realized how God had codded me, listening to my prayers for the safe return of this monster.

"Shut up, you!" I bawled, beside myself.

"What's that you said?" shouted Father, making a wild leap out of the bed.

"Mick, Mick!" cried Mother. "Don't you see the child isn't used to you?"

"I see he's better fed than taught," snarled Father, waving his arms wildly. "He wants his bottom smacked."

All his previous shouting was as nothing to these obscene words referring to my person. They really made my blood boil.

"Smack your own!" I screamed hysterically. "Smack your own! Shut up! Shut up!"

At this he lost his patience and let fly at me. He did it with the lack of conviction you'd expect of a man under Mother's horrified eyes, and it ended up as a mere tap, but the sheer indignity of being struck at all by a stranger, a total stranger who had cajoled his way back from the war into our big bed as a result of my innocent intercession, made me completely dotty. I shrieked and shrieked, and danced in my bare feet, and Father, looking awkward and hairy in nothing but a short gray army shirt, glared down at me like a mountain out for murder. I think it must have been then that I realized he was jealous too. And there stood Mother in her nightdress, looking as if her heart was broken between us. I hoped she felt as she looked. It seemed to me that she deserved it all.

From that morning out my life was a hell. Father and I were enemies, open and avowed. We conducted a series of skirmishes against one another, he trying to steal my time with Mother and I his. When she was sitting on my bed, telling me a story, he took to looking for some pair of old boots which he alleged he had left behind him at the beginning of the war. While he talked to Mother I played loudly with my toys to show my total lack of concern. He created a terrible scene one evening when he came in from work and found me at his box, playing with his regimental badges, Gurkha knives and button-sticks. Mother got up and took the box from me.

"You mustn't play with Daddy's toys unless he lets you, Larry," she said severely. "Daddy doesn't play with yours."

For some reason Father looked at her as if she had struck him and then turned away with a scowl.

"Those are not toys," he growled, taking down the box again to see had I lifted anything. "Some of those curios are very rare and valuable."

But as time went on I saw more and more how he managed to alienate Mother and me. What made it worse was that I couldn't grasp his method or see what attraction he had for Mother. In every possible way he was less winning than I. He had a common accent and made noises at his tea. I thought for a while that it might be the newspapers she was interested in, so I made up bits of news of my own to read to her. Then I thought it might be the smoking, which I personally thought attractive, and took his pipes and went round the house dribbling into them till he caught me. I even made noises at my tea, but Mother only told me I was disgusting. It all seemed to hinge round that unhealthy habit of sleeping together, so I made a point of dropping into their bedroom and nosing round, talking to myself, so that they wouldn't know I was watching them, but they were never up to anything that I could see. In the end it beat me. It seemed to depend on being grown-up and giving people rings, and I realized I'd have to wait.

But at the same time I wanted him to see that I was only waiting, not giving up the fight. One evening when he was being particularly obnoxious, chattering away well above my head, I let him have it.

"Mummy," I said, "do you know what I'm going to do when I grow up?"

"No, dear," she replied. "What?"

"I'm going to marry you," I said quietly.

Father gave a great guffaw out of him, but he didn't take me in. I knew it must only be pretense. And Mother, in spite of everything, was pleased. I felt she was probably relieved to know that one day Father's hold on her would be broken.

"Won't that be nice?" she said with a smile.

"It'll be very nice," I said confidently. "Because we're going to have lots and lots of babies."

"That's right, dear," she said placidly. "I think we'll have one soon, and then you'll have plenty of company."

I was no end pleased about that because it showed that in spite of the way she gave in to Father she still considered my wishes. Besides, it would put the Geneys in their place.

It didn't turn out like that, though. To begin with, she was very preoccupied—I supposed about where she would get the seventeen and six—and though Father took to staying out late in the evenings it did me no particular good. She stopped taking me for walks, became as touchy as blazes, and smacked me for nothing at all. Sometimes I wished I'd never mentioned the confounded baby—I seemed to have a genius for bringing calamity on myself.

And calamity it was! Sonny arrived in the most appalling hullabaloo—even that much he couldn't do without a fuss—and from the first moment I disliked him. He was a difficult child—so far as I was concerned he was always difficult—and demanded far too much attention. Mother was simply silly about him, and couldn't see when he was only showing off. As company he was worse than useless. He slept all day, and I had to go round the house on tiptoe to avoid waking him. It wasn't any longer a question of not waking Father. The slogan now was "Don't-wake-Sonny!" I couldn't understand why the child wouldn't sleep at the proper time, so whenever Mother's back was turned I woke him. Sometimes to keep him awake I pinched him as well. Mother caught me at it one day and gave me a most unmerciful flaking.

One evening, when Father was coming in from work, I was playing trains in the front garden. I let on not to notice him; instead, I pretended to be talking to myself, and said in a loud voice: "If another bloody baby comes into this house, I'm going out."

Father stopped dead and looked at me over his shoulder.

"What's that you said?" he asked sternly.

"I was only talking to myself," I replied, trying to conceal my panic. "It's private."

He turned and went in without a word. Mind you, I intended it as a solemn warning, but its effect was quite different. Father started being quite nice to me. I could understand that, of course. Mother was quite sickening about Sonny. Even at mealtimes she'd get up and gawk at him in the cradle with an idiotic smile, and tell Father to do the same. He was always polite about it, but he looked so puzzled you could see he didn't know what she was talking about. He complained of the way Sonny cried at night, but she only got cross and said that Sonny never cried except when there was something up with him—which was a flaming lie, because Sonny never had anything up with him, and only cried for attention. It was really painful to see how simpleminded she was. Father wasn't attractive, but he had a fine intelligence. He saw through Sonny, and now he knew that I saw through him as well.

One night I woke with a start. There was someone beside me in the bed. For one wild moment I felt sure it must be Mother, having come to her senses and left Father for good, but then I heard Sonny in convulsions in the next room, and Mother saying: "There! There! There!" and I knew it wasn't she. It was Father. He was lying beside me, wide awake, breathing hard and apparently as mad as hell.

After a while it came to me what he was mad about. It was his turn now. After turning me out of the big bed, he had been turned out himself. Mother had no consideration now for anyone but that poisonous pup, Sonny. I couldn't help feeling sorry for Father. I had been through it all myself, and even at that age I was magnanimous. I began to stroke him down and say: "There! There!" He wasn't exactly responsive.

"Aren't you asleep either?" he snarled.

"Ah, come on and put your arm around us, can't you?"

I said, and he did, in a sort of way. Gingerly, I suppose, is how you'd describe it. He was very bony but better than nothing.

At Christmas he went out of his way to buy me a really nice model railway.

Women and Children First

Francine Prose

Gordie likes to say he can read the writing on the wall: Soon armies of upscale D.C. couples will be buying second homes in quaint Monterey County, driving property values sky high. They've already *done* the Blue Ridge. Janet rents a farmhouse in Monterey and trucks in antiques, which Gordie sells at American Beauty, his Georgetown shop. Gordie says that renters in Monterey will soon be dinosaurs in museums. Janet can't quite believe that the moving finger is writing about real estate, but she knows that with Gordie prophecy is a form of advice: lately, he has been saying that she should buy some failing cracker-barrel mom-and-pop store and turn it into American Beauty West.

They have just smoked a joint in Gordie's bedroom, in the basement of his shop. They are sitting cross-legged on his carved fourposter bed, amid the Chinese knickknacks, the Oscar Wilde bearskin rug, the moth-eaten taxidermy that Gordie says is illegal even to own, and looking through a carton of antique nursery-rhyme illustrations—the remnants of some disintegrated kids' book that someone recognized as beautiful and worth saving. Janet found it yesterday at an estate sale in Slate Mills.

Janet turns a cardboard wheel, and beneath a cutout window a cow jumps over the moon. Next comes the laughing dog, the hand-in-hand dish and spoon. Gordie says, "These are a gold mine. I can frame them—the perfect new-baby gift. Sure you don't want to steal a couple for Kevin's room?"

"Kevin?" says Janet. "Gordie, this is 'Hey Diddle Diddle.' Kevin's got Tina Turner on his wall."

"*I* had Tina Turner on *my* wall," Gordie says. "Well, anyway, Ike."

Janet would like to keep the page she is holding, but her work gives her daily instruction in letting go. It would be easy for her to accumulate objects, to be buried beneath them. Yesterday she wondered how the elderly brother and sister who had come to supervise the estate sale, the disposal of their parents' things, could sell these pictures at all: their childhood fantasy images, a dollar for the whole box. She kept reminding herself that there was a lesson here—that basically they were right.

"I'll tell you something weird," she says. "Last night I was spinning this 'Hey Diddle Diddle' wheel, just looking at it. Kevin was upstairs asleep. After a while I heard him come down. He said he'd had a great dream about a flying cow."

Gordie says, "Could he have seen the picture?," and when Janet shakes her head he says, "You really should get this checked out." This sounds like medical advice, which in a way it is. Gordie says he has a friend at Georgetown Medical School who told him that someone there has gotten a small grant to study family ESP. What friend, wonders Janet. Gordie often uses the word to mean some guy he found attractive and maybe even had a long conversation with at a bar.

Janet says she'll ask Kevin; she knows he'll never agree. Kevin takes it for granted that he and Janet have the same thoughts; he can't understand why Janet gets so excited about it. Maybe he worries that thinking like a girl means you are one. He says that all kids and parents think alike; it's just from living in the same house, and if it doesn't happen with his father it's only because Will doesn't live with them but in D.C. When Janet asks Kevin if he has talked to other kids about this, he says, "Are you crazy?" What, then, would he think of scientists getting grants to ask other parents and kids? He'd think it was weird, and, worse, he'd know that it would involve every kind of attention he hates.

Just before Janet leaves Georgetown, Gordie asks if she doesn't at least want to keep the cow jumping over the moon. Janet makes a little sweep with her hand. "Gordie," she says, "I'm just a conduit. Hear the wind blowing through?"

On the drive back to Monterey, Janet keeps looking in her rearview mirror, imagining Gordie's armies—convoys of house-hunting Volvos and Saabs bearing down on her. Nearly home, she stops for a couple of hitchhikers—local characters, old hippies Kevin refers to as Mr. Time Travel and his wife. Janet has picked them up a few times before and does so again today, because Mrs. Time Travel appears to be hugely pregnant.

When the man helps his wife into the cab of the truck, Janet smells patchouli. The woman is overweight to begin with, but her husband is very bony; it averages out, and they fit fairly comfortably on the front seat. As Janet drives them into Staunton, Mr. Time Travel tells her how their welfare worker is threatening to cut them off if his wife doesn't get to a doctor. He talks very softly about the horrors of hospital birth—women trussed up and drugged, bright lights shining in babies' eyes—and every time he says "trussed up" Janet feels his wife flinch.

Something about this conversation makes Janet determined to bring Kevin in for the ESP experiments. Maybe it's the impulse to distinguish herself from *these* dinosaurs, to identify herself as the modern, if downwardly mobile, former wife of a surgeon and the mother of a perfectly healthy hospital-born kid. Partly, she just longs for something new. When she and Will split up, and she found this way to live out here and make money, she'd thought that the rest of her life would be a treasure hunt. The auctions, the sales, checking the local obits—how quickly it all came to seem like a job! It's got so her heart sinks at the sight of another beautiful oak hutch. Also she wonders if this new desire to be a famous ESP guinea pig is just that old dream of specialness, of celebrity and revenge: mind-reading mom and kid amazing talk-show hosts, written up by Oliver Sacks, so even Will will read about it.

She wants to just do it—just go there for the experiments and not argue—so that night at dinner she tells Kevin that if he comes with her, no questions asked, he can have a new baseball mitt and two computer games.

"Medical school?" Kevin says.

"Trust me," says Janet, and they both smile, because

this is Kevin's expression. "No doctors," she says. "Looking at pictures. ESP experiments. That kind of thing. O.K., listen. They'll pay us ten dollars an hour, you get to keep the money."

"Ten dollars an hour?" he repeats, and when Janet nods he says, "That and the ant farm." Lately he has been asking for an ant farm; she should have thought of that right away. Where did he hear about ant farms? And where in the world do you get one? Tracking down items from science-museum shops is not the kind of thing either she or Will does well, especially not now, with Will spending every free minute with his new girlfriend. And the way Kevin takes care of things there's a good chance that dirt, broken glass, and a million ants will wind up on his bedroom floor. Still, she says, "O.K., the ant farm."

Janet makes an appointment at the medical school for a Wednesday; she tells Kevin he'll learn as much as he would have from two days at school. At one time he liked missing school, no matter what. But now he's clearly torn, and on the day of the appointment Janet feels so guilty that she stops, without his even asking, for a takeout McDonald's breakfast. As they merge with a stream of trucks on Route 74, she says, "In a few years, you'll be driving. It seems impossible—you were just this little baby."

After a long silence, Kevin says, "Do you have to catch the ants, or can you just buy them somewhere?"

"I don't know," Janet says. "I'll find out."

And that's it for conversation. For most of the drive, Kevin stares out the window. Glancing over at him, Janet thinks how soon he will be a teenager; now he is right on the edge. It occurs to her that being so handsome may make it easier for him, but she can't tell him this; it is already too late.

She pulls into the Park 'n' Ride Lot, where Gordie is already waiting. His emerald '56 Buick gleams like a giant eight-cylinder scarab. Janet is glad to see him, glad that he offered to close the store and come with them. She loves riding in Gordie's car: everyone turns to look at you as you sink into the deep sofa-like seats and breathe in the stuffy, indescribable smell of your childhood. Gordie said he wanted to expedite their trip, to free their minds for higher things, but Janet suspects that he'd like to run into his friend at the medical school.

The waiting room reminds her of an expensive obstetrician's—in fact, of the office of the old man Will knew who delivered Kevin for free. It's smaller, of course, and empty, but even so Janet has that waiting-room self-consciousness as she sits between Kevin, with his punky baseball cap pulled over his eyes, and Gordie, with his ginger mustache and leather bomber jacket; as if there were someone there watching, she feels proud to be sitting between them. Kevin likes Gordie, though he spends too much time with Will and his doctor/intellectual friends to give Gordie much credit as a full-scale human adult. Gordie has brought Kevin treasures—special marbles, a rooster-shaped tin bank, a revolving lamp with a scene of Niagara Falls—which Kevin seems to like but leaves all over his room.

After a while, a receptionist calls Janet and Kevin. Gordie says, "Adios and good luck. If I'm not here, I'm taking a walk. I'll be back." The receptionist, a barrel-like young woman, takes off down the scratchy-industrial-carpeted hall; Janet and Kevin fly after her, and so have to brake sharply when she motions them through an office door.

Inside, a woman sits behind a desk, a man in a chair

beside her. The woman is wearing a lab coat. Janet wonders why she needs it; she'd always thought lab coats were to guard against spraying mouse blood. The man and the woman stand to shake hands. They are both around Janet's age—a fact that horrifies her, and convinces her that she shouldn't have come. She feels humiliated, as if being on the opposite side of this scientific investigation is an admission of failure in life.

The woman introduces herself as Dr. Wilmot. She is tall, a light-skinned black, with huge, stylish eyeglasses, a clear, lively smile, and unruly half-straight hair. She introduces the man as Dr. Becker, and he laughs and says, "Eric." He is good-looking in that clean, academic way that can make jeans and rolled shirtsleeves look like a lab coat—not clinical, exactly, just terribly pressed and neat. When Eric shakes Janet's hand, he smiles and looks at her closely. She focuses on a postcard tacked to the corkboard on the wall behind him—a vintage anthropological photograph of two Pygmy women playing Ping-Pong.

Dr. Wilmot says she'd like to say a little about their study. She says they are lucky—there's really no money around for this kind of project these days. She says the experiment is simply the classic model: they'll be put in separate rooms and asked to look at pictures. She asks if they have any questions. Janet can't think of one. Kevin looks too bored to speak.

They leave Dr. Wilmot's office and walk awkwardly down the hall; no one knows whom to walk with. After a while they reach two open doors. Dr. Wilmot motions Janet and Eric into one room, and she and Kevin take the other. Janet realizes how glad she is that it's not the other way round, and she wonders if this arrangement is accidental or if research has discovered that ESP gets sharper around a slight sexual buzz.

As Kevin disappears through the door, Dr. Wilmot smiles encouragingly but with a certain strain, so that it comes out almost a leer. Janet feels strange, as if she were involving her child in something scandalous, like some Victorian father introducing his son to the local bordello.

The room Eric takes her into is dimly lit, bare but for two wooden chairs and a wooden table, rather like the set of a low-budget avant-garde play. On the table is a deck of cards, face down, and a clipboard and pen. Eric picks up the clipboard and says he is sorry, he has to take a history. Again Janet has a flash of the obstetrician's, more panicky now, but at least he doesn't ask when she got chicken pox or her first period—facts she has long since forgotten and so always has to reinvent. He asks about traumatic childhood illnesses or experiences, hers and Kevin's. Janet says, "Normal. . . . Normal. . . . Normal." Finally he asks, "When was the first time you sensed some special connection with your son?"

"Special connection?" she says.

Eric's gesture takes in the room. "You know," he says.

"Do you have kids?" asks Janet. Eric jumps slightly, then says, "Three. They live with their mother. I get them alternate weekends." He says this with some bewilderment, as if he hadn't yet figured out why it should be. Janet finds that encouraging, and goes back to considering his question. Special connection? There was that night just before she went into labor, when the baby's kicking woke her up and she knew—she just knew—he was miserable, he didn't want to be born. But maybe mentioning this will label her right from the start as an unreliable subject.

So she tells him about the first incident actually witnessed by bona-fide-scientist Will. "This is a crazy story," she says. Eric moves his chair nearer hers. "I was breaking up with my husband. At that time I thought I'd stay in D.C. For Kevin. Will was helping me find an apartment. The first place we saw was full of eyeballs. Everywhere—the kitchen counter, the toilet tank, every surface was covered with Plasticine eyeballs. It turned out that the woman who lived there made models for a medical-supply house and she'd gotten a big order. My husband is a doctor; they'd used models like that in medical school, so they had lots to talk about. I knew I couldn't live there, even though she was taking the eyeballs with her, and on the way home my husband and I had a fight, because otherwise it was a perfectly good apartment, and why was I being so squeamish? We picked Kevin up at my friend's. And *she* was in a bad mood because her kid was Kevin's age and couldn't draw a straight line and Kevin had spent the whole afternoon drawing these perfect eyeballs."

"Wow," Eric says. "Is that really true?"

"Every word," says Janet, though she's left out the fact that the eyeball-apartment woman was young and pretty.

"How did your husband feel about it?" Eric asks.

"He hated it. He acted like I did it on purpose—coached Kevin. I stopped telling him when things like that happened, but sometimes, when they happened in front of him, he used to say he felt like an actor in one of those disaster movies with the Titanic sinking and everyone yelling 'Women and children first!,' except that his wife and kid had already gone and left him standing on deck, watching their lifeboat float off."

Janet realizes she has never told even Gordie about Will's saying this. She mentioned it only once, drunk, at a D.C. party. Someone was talking about the actual Titanic, and she stopped the whole conversation by quoting Will. There was a terrible silence, till finally some lefty lawyer type said something lame and solemn—meant nonetheless as a halfhearted come-on—about the whole male sex being stuck on a sinking ship.

"I used to feel awful when he'd say that," Janet says. "I'd think, Hey, he's a doctor, he has enough in his life without envying me and Kevin. But I don't know. I guess he felt left out; I guess everybody wants everything."

Janet pauses, slightly embarrassed and pleased that saying "everybody wants everything" may have made her sound like a greedy slave of appetite. She doubts that it's even true. One night last fall, when Kevin was in D.C., Janet went home with a man—a candlemaker—she met at a Charlottesville crafts fair. After a while, he showed her into his bedroom; he'd lit mushroom candles all over. Though touched by his attempt at romance, she was appalled by those hideous glowing mushrooms, and she couldn't go through with it; she excused herself and left.

What she wants to tell Eric is how, in the end, Will was really the prescient one. Because finally, wasn't he right? Janet and Kevin in one boat, Will in another, an ocean—all right, a highway—between them. Sometimes it astonishes her that her strongest—her only—connection is with a child; it's common enough, she knows, but not what she expected. And now, when she imagines those disaster films, it's the women's faces she sees, the looks on their faces as they climb down into the boats: fear mixed with amazement that when the order came they so readily, so instinctively, complied. But saying this might make her life with Kevin sound impenetrable, closed off, full up. It's why, she sometimes thinks, she's so adamant about not accumulating lots of stuff. What man wouldn't hesitate in the doorway of a house where a woman and child live surrounded by perfect antiques?

Eric says, "Was that part of what came between you?"

"The tiniest part," she says. Then they both fall silent. Janet remembers a magazine article that claimed that one sign of sexual interest is the reflected gesture: she picks up a glass, he picks up a glass, he crosses his legs, so does she. She hopes that shared silence counts. She thinks about Kevin and Dr. Wilmot on the other side of the wall: if she asked Kevin for history, they would have finished long ago. Then a red darkroom light blinks on the wall, and Eric says, "Here's the story. Simple geometric images—triangles, squares. We're trying to eliminate the variables."

Janet is disappointed: the experiments she has read about used images like camels in the desert, the Alamo, rockets in outer space. But maybe that's why they never got conclusive results. Eric explains that in the first round Kevin will send, Janet receive. He tells Janet to close her eyes and concentrate, and call out whatever comes to mind. Janet imagines triangles, squares. They all seem equally likely. None of them flash on and off or in any other way signal her as beaming from Kevin's brain.

Her only thoughts are of Eric, how conscious she is of him awaiting her answer; she desperately wants to do well. She thinks that everything is backward: Here she is, going through this with her kid, and the only telepathy she cares about is with the guy running the test. It's hopelessly distracting, but when it's her turn to send, things seem somewhat easier. She fixes her eyes on the triangle and wonders if Kevin will blame her for making him do yet another boring thing that she'd thought would be fun.

Finally Eric says, "Well, that's it." They look at each other a moment too long. Janet looks away. There's some complicated timing here, much more finely tuned than who picks up the wineglass first. They leave the room together; Dr. Wilmot and Kevin are already in the hall. When Kevin pouts, as he's doing now, he looks like a much younger kid. Janet has a moment of hating herself for the disloyalty of dragging Kevin here, making him sit through this, and, on top of all that, wishing he would act friendlier for some guy she has just met.

Dr. Wilmot asks if Janet and Kevin will bear with them for just a few more minutes in the waiting room. Janet and Eric exchange a quick, heavy look, embarrassingly reminiscent of suburban-adultery movies. Janet says, "No problem."

Gordie glances up when they enter, and, for a moment, Janet wonders what he's doing there. He looks so out of context, so far from the Victorian burgundy reds of his bedroom. "How was it?" he says.

"Tons of fun," says Kevin.

Janet is about to ask Gordie if he met up with his friend when Dr. Wilmot and Eric walk in.

"Eric," says Gordie.

Eric looks a little blankly at Gordie, then says, "Oh, hi."

"You guys know each other?" says Janet. Eric looks from Janet to Gordie, somehow managing to pay them both that same serious attention Janet felt from him back in the room. Well, you can never tell. Janet reminds herself not to jump to conclusions. Eric might not even be gay; Gordie is always developing these sudden impossible crushes.

Dr. Wilmot tells them that the final results aren't in yet but right now the quick matchups indicate an unusually high score, at least in one direction—Janet sending, Kevin receiving.

Janet feels wronged: in fact she knows Kevin's thoughts as often as he knows hers. She has a childish desire to say that it's Eric's fault, for ruining her concentration. But she can only smile lamely as Dr. Wilmot says she'll be in touch with them about followup tests, and can expect payment shortly. "The check's in the mail," she says, and they all laugh. Everyone says good-bye and shakes hands except Kevin, who stands in the doorway, impatiently rolling his eyes.

On the way to the car, Kevin walks up ahead. "Watch out, it's a parking lot," calls Janet.

Gordie says, "What do you think about Eric?"

"Very cute," says Janet.

"No," says Gordie. "I mean, you're the one with ESP. Do you think he's gay?"

Janet should be cheered by this. Maybe there is some basis to whatever she felt in that room—maybe Eric will call, maybe anything else is in Gordie's mind. Then she remembers how Eric looked at them—both of them. She thinks, Maybe Eric is just your basic compulsive seducer. Suddenly she feels exhausted. It occurs to her that if you heard what was said in any hospital parking lot, on any average day, you would hear lots of bad news. And now she can't bring herself to give Gordie one bit more. "Yes," she says. "I do. He couldn't keep his eyes off you."

"Really?" says Gordie.

"Trust me," says Janet.

They find Kevin sitting on the hood of Gordie's car, his long legs dangling. He gets in back, and Janet slides in beside Gordie.

A block from the hospital, Gordie stops at a crosswalk and waves some pedestrians across—an Italian or Hispanic family, formally dressed, walking slowly so as to wait for a little girl in a white Communion dress who is limping, straggling behind, stopping every few minutes to pop her little white pump off her heel and lift her foot and examine it. Even from the car, Janet can see the angry red blister on the girl's heel. Suddenly she wishes Will were there—or maybe not Will, just someone, a husband or lover she trusted to know what she couldn't begin to say about that little girl, that white dress, that blister.

From the back seat, Kevin says, "What's the point of having ESP if you can't tell when girls like you?"

He sounds furious, and this surprises Janet more than what he has said, or that he should have said it at all. There's a silence. Finally Gordie says, "Good question."

Janet knows she could blow the moment completely by asking "Like who? Like which girl?" She takes a deep breath before she says, "Well, you can. A lot of times you can. You just learn how, that's all."

"How?" Kevin says.

"Take your father," Janet says. "We were eating in a restaurant with these friends who were introducing us—"

"Who?" asks Kevin.

"You didn't know them," she says. "They moved when you were little. They had a kid they let run *everything*—he even got to pick the restaurant. So we ate at a diner he liked because it had mirrored walls. But that night he didn't care about the walls. He wouldn't sit in his chair; he ran around, getting under the waitresses' feet, and our friends kept having to jump up and drag him back. Each time, one of them would say, 'You go, I went last time,' so things were a little tense. From time to time they'd tease Will about having a kid, having to do what *they* were doing; I guess he had a reputation for not liking kids. Finally Will called the kid over and sat him down between us—we were on the same side of the booth. Will cut the kid's hamburger up for him, in little pieces; the kid was so surprised that he quieted down and ate his whole meal. Our friends didn't say a word. They must have been wondering what had come over your dad. But I knew he was doing it for me—to show me he was the kind of guy who could be nice to kids."

"Right," says Kevin.

Janet thinks, Right about what?, but lets it go. Will was always nice to Kevin, or, anyway, an acceptable balance of nice and not nice, no more or less nice than she was. Anyway, she just wants to sit and remember that night in the restaurant—not the noisy kid or the bickering parents but this: how Will's hands shook as he sawed away at that burger, and how she had thought here was a surgeon, a man with steady hands, and look, look what power she had.

"Aren't you ever wrong?" Kevin says.

Gordie says, "Not about that. If there's one thing your mom's psychic about, it's that."

Janet looks out the window. They're almost at the Park 'n' Ride, where she left the truck; she wishes she'd used the bathroom in the medical school. There are only gas stations from here on out. She has always been a little scared of public bathrooms—except when she was pregnant with Kevin. Nothing scared her then. She had company.

They say goodbye to Gordie and drive off. A few miles past the beltway, Kevin says, "Could you pull over somewhere?"

Janet drives onto the shoulder, and Kevin climbs down from the truck. As he heads toward the edge of the woods, he keeps stopping, crouching down. It takes her a while to figure out: he's looking for ants. She watches till he's hidden by trees and she can no longer see him.

It seems like a long time till he reappears, and though she tells herself that nothing could have happened, she is beginning to get anxious when she spots his blue baseball cap. Emerging from the woods, he waves at her—a broad, enthusiastic wave, as if from miles away.

The Leap

Louise Erdrich

My mother is the surviving half of a blindfold trapeze act, not a fact I think about much even now that she is sightless, the result of encroaching and stubborn cataracts. She walks slowly through her house here in New Hampshire, lightly touching her way along walls and running her hands over knickknacks, books, the drift of a grown child's belongings and castoffs. She has never upset an object or as much as brushed a magazine onto the floor. She has never lost her balance or bumped into a closet door left carelessly open.

It has occurred to me that the catlike precision of her movements in old age might be the result of her early training, but she shows so little of the drama or flair one might expect from a performer that I tend to forget the Flying Avalons. She has kept no sequined costume, no photographs, no fliers or posters from that part of her youth. I would, in fact, tend to think that all memory of double somersaults and heartstopping catches had left her arms and legs were it not for the fact that sometimes, as I sit sewing in the room of the rebuilt house in which I slept as a child, I hear the crackle, catch a whiff of smoke from the stove downstairs, and suddenly the room goes dark, the stitches burn beneath my fingers, and I am sewing with a needle of hot silver, a thread of fire.

I owe her my existence three times. The first was when she saved herself. In the town square a replica tent pole, cracked and splintered, now stands cast in concrete. It commemorates the disaster that put our town smack on the front page of the Boston and New York tabloids. It is from those old newspapers, now historical records, that I get my information. Not from my mother, Anna of the Flying Avalons, nor from any of her in-laws, nor certainly from the other half of her particular act, Harold Avalon, her first husband. In one news account it says, "The day was mildly overcast, but nothing in the air or temperature gave any hint of the sudden force with which the deadly gale would strike."

I have lived in the West, where you can see the weather coming for miles, and it is true that out here we are at something of a disadvantage. When extremes of temperature collide, a hot and cold front, winds generate instantaneously behind a hill and crash upon you without warning. That, I think, was the likely situation on that day in June. People probably commented on the pleasant air, grateful that no hot sun beat upon the striped tent that stretched over the entire center green. They bought their tickets and surrendered them in anticipation. They sat. They ate caramelized popcorn and roasted peanuts. There was time, before the storm, for three acts. The White Arabians of Ali-Khazar rose on their hind legs and waltzed. The Mysterious Bernie folded himself into a painted cracker tin, and the Lady of the Mists made herself appear and disappear in surprising places. As the clouds gathered outside, unnoticed, the ringmaster cracked his whip, shouted his introduction, and pointed to the ceiling of the tent, where the Flying Avalons were perched.

They loved to drop gracefully from nowhere, like two sparkling birds, and blow kisses as they threw off their plumed helmets and high-collared capes. They laughed and flirted openly as they beat their way up again on the trapeze bars. In the final vignette of their act, they actually would kiss in midair, pausing, almost hovering as they swooped past one another. On the ground, between bows, Harry Avalon would skip quickly to the front rows and point out the smear of my mother's lipstick, just off the edge of his mouth. They made a romantic pair all right, especially in the blindfold sequence.

That afternoon, as the anticipation increased, as Mr. and Mrs. Avalon tied sparkling strips of cloth onto each other's face and as they puckered their lips in mock kisses, lips destined "never again to meet," as one long breathless article put it, the wind rose, miles off, wrapped itself into a cone, and howled. There came a rumble of electrical energy, drowned out by the sudden roll of drums. One detail not mentioned by the press, perhaps unknown—Anna was pregnant at the time, seven months and hardly showing, her stomach muscles were that strong. It seems incredible that she would work high above the ground when any fall could be so dangerous, but the explanation—I know from watching her go blind—is that my mother lives comfortably in extreme elements. She is one with the constant dark now, just as the air was her home, familiar to her, safe, before the storm that afternoon.

From opposite ends of the tent they waved, blind and smiling, to the crowd below. The ringmaster removed his hat and called for silence, so that the two above could concentrate. They rubbed their hands in chalky powder, then Harry launched himself and swung, once, twice, in huge calibrated beats across space. He hung from his knees and on the third swing stretched wide his arms, held his hands out to receive his pregnant wife as she dove from her shining bar.

It was while the two were in midair, their hands about to meet, that lightning struck the main pole and sizzled down the guy wires, filling the air with a blue radiance that Harry Avalon must certainly have seen through the cloth of his blindfold as the tent buckled and the edifice toppled him forward, the swing continuing and not returning in its sweep, and Harry going down, down into the crowd with his last thought, perhaps, just a prickle of surprise at his empty hands.

My mother once said that I'd be amazed at how many things a person can do within the act of falling. Perhaps, at the time, she was teaching me to dive off a board at the town pool, for I associate the idea with midair somersaults. But I also think she meant that even in that awful doomed second one could think, for she certainly did. When her hands did not meet her husband's, my mother tore her blindfold away. As he swept past her on the wrong side, she could have grasped his ankle, the toe-end of his tights, and gone down clutching him. Instead, she changed direction. Her body twisted toward a heavy wire and she managed to hang on to the braided metal, still hot from the lightning strike. Her palms were burned so terribly that once healed they bore no lines, only the blank scar tissue of a quieter future. She was lowered, gently, to the sawdust ring just underneath the dome of the canvas roof, which did not entirely settle but was held up on one end and jabbed through, torn, and still on fire in places from the giant spark, though rain and men's jackets soon put that out.

Three people died, but except for her hands my mother was not seriously harmed until an overeager rescuer broke her arm in extricating her and also, in the process, collapsed a portion of the tent bearing a huge buckle that knocked her unconscious. She was taken to the town hospital, and there she must have hemorrhaged, for they kept her, confined to her bed, a month and a half before her baby was born without life.

Harry Avalon had wanted to be buried in the circus cemetery next to the original Avalon, his uncle, so she sent him back with his brothers. The child, however, is buried around the corner, beyond this house and just down the highway. Sometimes I used to walk there just to sit. She was a girl, but I rarely thought of her as a sister or even as a separate person really. I suppose you could call it the egocentrism of a child, of all young children, but I considered her a less finished version of myself.

When the snow falls, throwing shadows among the stones, I can easily pick hers out from the road, for it is bigger than the others and in the shape of a lamb at rest, its legs curled beneath. The carved lamb looms larger as the years pass, though it is probably only my eyes, the vision shifting, as what is close to me blurs and distances sharpen. In odd moments, I think it is the edge drawing near, the edge of everything, the unseen horizon we do not really speak of in the eastern woods. And it also seems to me, although this is probably an idle fantasy, that the statue is growing more sharply etched, as if, instead of weathering itself into a porous mass, it is hardening on the hillside with each snowfall, perfecting itself.

It was during her confinement in the hospital that my mother met my father. He was called in to look at the set of her arm, which was complicated. He stayed, sitting at her bedside, for he was something of an armchair traveler and had spent his war quietly, at an air force training grounds, where he became a specialist in arms and legs broken during parachute training exercises. Anna Avalon had been to many of the places he longed to visit—Venice, Rome, Mexico, all through France and Spain. She had no family of her own and was taken in by the Avalons, trained to perform from a very young age. They toured Europe before the war, then based themselves in New York. She was illiterate.

It was in the hospital that she finally learned to read and write, as a way of overcoming the boredom and depression of those weeks, and it was my father who insisted on teaching her. In return for stories of her adventures, he graded her first exercises. He bought her her first book, and over her bold letters, which the pale guides of the penmanship pads could not contain, they fell in love.

I wonder if my father calculated the exchange he offered: one form of flight for another. For after that, and for as long as I can remember, my mother has never been without a book. Until now, that is, and it remains the greatest difficulty of her blindness. Since my father's recent death, there is no one to read to her, which is why I returned, in fact, from my failed life where the land is flat. I came home to read to my mother, to read out loud, to read long into the dark if I must, to read all night.

Once my father and mother married, they moved onto the old farm he had inherited but didn't care much for. Though he'd been thinking of moving to a larger city, he settled down and broadened his practice in this valley. It still seems odd to me, when they could have gone anywhere else, that they chose to stay in the town where the disaster had occurred, and which my father in the first place had found so constricting. It was my mother who insisted upon it, after her child did not survive. And then, too, she loved the sagging farmhouse with its scrap of what was left of a vast acreage of woods and hidden hay fields that stretched to the game park.

I owe my existence, the second time then, to the two of them and the hospital that brought them together. That is the debt we take for granted since none of us asks for life. It is only once we have it that we hang on so dearly.

I was seven the year the house caught fire, probably from standing ash. It can rekindle, and my father, forgetful around the house and perpetually exhausted from night hours on call, often emptied what he thought were ashes from cold stoves into wooden or cardboard containers. The fire could have started from a flaming box, or perhaps a buildup of creosote inside the chimney was the culprit. It started right around the stove, and the heart of the house was gutted. The baby-sitter, fallen asleep in my father's den on the first floor, woke to find the stairway to my upstairs room cut off by flames. She used the phone, then ran outside to stand beneath my window.

When my parents arrived, the town volunteers had drawn water from the fire pond and were spraying the outside of the house, preparing to go inside after me, not knowing at the time that there was only one staircase and that it was lost. On the other side of the house, the superannuated extension ladder broke in half. Perhaps the clatter of it falling against the walls woke me, for I'd been asleep up to that point.

As soon as I awakened, in the small room that I now use for sewing, I smelled the smoke. I followed things by the letter then, was good at memorizing instructions, and so I did exactly what was taught in the second-grade home fire drill. I got up, I touched the back of my door before opening it. Finding it hot, I left it closed and stuffed my rolled-up rug beneath the crack. I did not hide under my bed or crawl into my closet. I put on my flannel robe, and then I sat down to wait.

Outside, my mother stood below my dark window and saw clearly that there was no rescue. Flames had pierced one side wall, and the glare of the fire lighted the massive limbs and trunk of the vigorous old elm that had probably been planted the year the house was built, a hundred years ago at least. No leaf touched the wall, and just one thin branch scraped the roof. From below, it looked as though even a squirrel would have had trouble jumping from the tree onto the house, for the breadth of that small branch was no bigger than my mother's wrist.

Standing there, beside Father, who was preparing to rush back around to the front of the house, my mother asked him to unzip her dress. When he wouldn't be bothered, she made him understand. He couldn't make his hands work, so she finally tore it off and stood there in her pearls and stockings. She directed one of the men to lean the broken half of the extension ladder up against the trunk of the tree. In surprise, he complied. She ascended. She vanished. Then she could be seen among the leafless branches of late November as she made her way up and, along her stomach, inched the length of a bough that curved above the branch that brushed the roof.

Once there, swaying, she stood and balanced. There were plenty of people in the crowd and many who still remember, or think they do, my mother's leap through the ice-dark air toward that thinnest extension, and how she broke the branch falling so that it cracked in her hands, cracked louder than the flames as she vaulted with it toward the edge of the roof, and how it hurtled down end over end without her, and their eyes went up, again, to see where she had flown.

I didn't see her leap through air, only heard the sudden thump and looked out my window. She was hanging by the backs of her heels from the new gutter we had put in that year, and she was smiling. I was not surprised to see her, she was so matter-of-fact. She tapped on the window. I remember how she did it, too. It was the friendliest tap, a bit tentative, as if she was afraid she had arrived too early at a friend's house. Then she gestured at the latch, and when I opened the window she told me to raise it wider and prop it up with the stick so it wouldn't crush her fingers. She swung down, caught the ledge, and crawled through the opening. Once she was in my room, I realized she had on only underclothing, a bra of the heavy stitched cotton women used to wear and step-in, lace-trimmed drawers. I remember feeling light-headed, of course, terribly relieved, and then embarrassed for her to be seen by the crowd undressed.

I was still embarrassed as we flew out the window, toward earth, me in her lap, her toes pointed as we skimmed toward the painted target of the fire fighter's net.

I know that she's right. I knew it even then. As you fall there is time to think. Curled as I was, against her stomach, I was not startled by the cries of the crowd or the looming faces. The wind roared and beat its hot breath at our back, the flames whistled. I slowly wondered what would happen if we missed the circle or bounced out of it. Then I wrapped my hands around my mother's hands. I felt the brush of her lips and heard the beat of her heart in my ears, loud as thunder, long as the roll of drums.

Gravity

David Leavitt

Theo had a choice between a drug that would save his sight and a drug that would keep him alive, so he chose not to go blind. He stopped the pills and started the injections—these required the implantation of an unpleasant and painful catheter just above his heart—and within a few days the clouds in his eyes started to clear up; he could see again. He remembered going into New York City to a show with his mother, when he was twelve and didn't want to admit he needed glasses. "Can you read that?" she'd shouted, pointing to a Broadway marquee, and when he'd squinted, making out only one or two letters, she'd taken off her own glasses—harlequins with tiny rhinestones in the corners—and shoved them onto his face. The world came into focus, and he gasped, astonished at the precision around the edges of things, the legibility, the hard, sharp, colorful landscape. Sylvia had to squint through *Fiddler on the Roof* that day, but for Theo, his face masked by his mother's huge glasses, everything was as bright and vivid as a comic book. Even though people stared at him, and muttered things, Sylvia didn't care; he could *see.*

Because he was dying again, Theo moved back to his mother's house in New Jersey. The DHPG injections she took in stride—she'd seen her own mother through *her* dying, after all. Four times a day, with the equanimity of a nurse, she cleaned out the plastic tube implanted in his chest, inserted a sterilized hypodermic and slowly dripped the bag of sight-giving liquid into his veins. They endured this procedure silently, Sylvia sitting on the side of the hospital bed she'd rented for the duration of Theo's stay—his life, he sometimes thought—watching reruns of *I Love Lucy* or the news, while he tried not to think about the hard piece of pipe stuck into him, even though it was a constant reminder of how wide and unswimmable the gulf was becoming between him and the ever-receding shoreline of the well. And Sylvia was intricately cheerful. Each day she urged him to go out with her somewhere—to the library, or the little museum with the dinosaur replicas he'd been fond of as a child—and when his thinness and the cane drew stares, she'd maneuver him around the people who were staring, determined to shield him from whatever they might say or do. It had been the same that afternoon so many years ago, when she'd pushed him through a lobbyful of curious and laughing faces, determined that nothing should interfere with the spectacle of his seeing. What a pair they must have made, a boy in ugly glasses and a mother daring the world to say a word about it!

This warm, breezy afternoon in May they were shopping for revenge. "Your cousin Howard's engagement party is next month," Sylvia explained in the car. "A very nice girl from Livingston. I met her a few weeks ago, and really, she's a superior person."

"I'm glad," Theo said. "Congratulate Howie for me."

"Do you think you'll be up to going to the party?"

"I'm not sure. Would it be okay for me just to give him a gift?"

"You already have. A lovely silver tray, if I say so myself. The thank-you note's in the living room."

"Mom," Theo said, "why do you always have to—"

Sylvia honked her horn at a truck making an illegal left turn. "Better they should get something than no present at all, is what I say," she said. "But now, the problem is, *I* have to give Howie something, to be from me, and it better be good. It better be very, very good."

"Why?"

"Don't you remember that cheap little nothing Bibi gave you for your graduation? It was disgusting."

"I can't remember what she gave me."

"Of course you can't. It was a tacky pen-and-pencil set. Not even a real leather box. So naturally, it stands to reason that I have to get something truly spectacular for Howard's engagement. Something that will make Bibi blanch. Anyway, I think I've found just the thing, but I need your advice."

"Advice? Well, when my old roommate Nick got married, I gave him a garlic press. It cost five dollars and reflected exactly how much I felt, at that moment, our friendship was worth."

Sylvia laughed. "Clever. But my idea is much more brilliant, because it makes it possible for me to get back at

Bibi *and* give Howard the nice gift he and his girl deserve." She smiled, clearly pleased with herself. "Ah, you live and learn."

"You live," Theo said.

Sylvia blinked. "Well, look, here we are." She pulled the car into a handicapped-parking place on Morris Avenue and got out to help Theo, but he was already hoisting himself up out of his seat, using the door handle for leverage. "I can manage myself," he said with some irritation. Sylvia stepped back.

"Clearly one advantage to all this for you," Theo said, balancing on his cane, "is that it's suddenly so much easier to get a parking place."

"Oh Theo, please," Sylvia said. "Look, here's where we're going."

She leaned him into a gift shop filled with porcelain statuettes of Snow White and all seven of the dwarves, music boxes which, when you opened them, played "The Shadow of Your Smile," complicated-smelling potpourris in purple wall-papered boxes, and stuffed snakes you were supposed to push up against drafty windows and doors.

"Mrs. Greenman," said an expansive, gray-haired man in a cream-colored cardigan sweater. "Look who's here, Archie, it's Mrs. Greenman."

Another man, this one thinner and balding, but dressed in an identical cardigan, peered out from the back of the shop. "Hello there!" he said, smiling. He looked at Theo, and his expression changed.

"Mr. Sherman, Mr. Baker. This is my son, Theo."

"Hello," Mr. Sherman and Mr. Baker said. They didn't offer to shake hands.

"Are you here for that item we discussed last week?" Mr. Sherman asked.

"Yes," Sylvia said. "I want advice from my son here." She walked over to a large ridged crystal bowl, a very fifties sort of bowl, stalwart and square-jawed. "What do you think? Beautiful, isn't it?"

"Mom, to tell the truth, I think it's kind of ugly."

"Four hundred and twenty-five dollars," Sylvia said admiringly. "You have to feel it."

Then she picked up the big bowl and tossed it to Theo, like a football.

The gentlemen in the cardigan sweaters gasped and did not exhale. When Theo caught it, it sank his hands. His cane rattled as it hit the floor.

"That's heavy," Sylvia said, observing with satisfaction how the bowl had weighted Theo's arms down. "And where crystal is concerned, heavy is impressive."

She took the bowl back from him and carried it to the counter. Mr. Sherman was mopping his brow. Theo looked at the floor, still surprised not to see shards of glass around his feet.

Since no one else seemed to be volunteering, he bent over and picked up the cane.

"Four hundred and fifty-nine, with tax," Mr. Sherman said, his voice still a bit shaky, and a look of relish came over Sylvia's face as she pulled out her checkbook to pay. Behind the counter, Theo could see Mr. Baker put his hand on his forehead and cast his eyes to the ceiling.

It seemed Sylvia had been looking a long time for something like this, something heavy enough to leave an impression, yet so fragile it could make you sorry.

* * *

They headed back out to the car.

"Where can we go now?" Sylvia asked, as she got in. "There must be someplace else to go."

"Home," Theo said. "It's almost time for my medicine."

"Really? Oh. All right." She pulled on her seat belt, inserted the car key in the ignition and sat there.

For just a moment, but perceptibly, her face broke. She squeezed her eyes shut so tight the blue shadow on the lids cracked.

Almost as quickly she was back to normal again, and they were driving. "It's getting hotter," Sylvia said. "Shall I put on the air?"

"Sure," Theo said. He was thinking about the bowl, or more specifically, about how surprising its weight had been, pulling his hands down. For a while now he'd been worried about his mother, worried about what damage his illness might secretly be doing to her that of course she would never admit. On the surface things seemed all right. She still broiled herself a skinned chicken breast for dinner every night, still swam a mile and a half a day, still kept used teabags wrapped in foil in the refrigerator. Yet she had also, at about three o'clock one morning, woken him up to tell him she was going to the twenty-four-hour supermarket, and was there anything he wanted. Then there was the gift shop: She had literally pitched that bowl toward him, pitched it like a ball, and as that great gleam of flight and potential regret came sailing his direction, it had occurred to him that she was trusting his two feeble hands, out of the whole world, to keep it from shattering. What was she trying to test? Was it his newly regained vision? Was it the assurance that he was there, alive, that he hadn't yet slipped past all her caring, a little lost boy in rhinestone-studded glasses? There are certain things you've already done before you even think how to do them—a child pulled from in front of a car, for instance, or the bowl, which Theo was holding before he could even begin to calculate its brief trajectory. It had pulled his arms down, and from that apish posture he'd looked at his mother, who smiled broadly, as if, in the war between heaviness and shattering, he'd just helped her win some small but sustaining victory.

Everyday Use

Alice Walker

FOR YOUR GRANDMAMMA

I will wait for her in the yard that Maggie and I made so clean and wavy yesterday afternoon. A yard like this is more comfortable than most people know. It is not just a yard. It is like an extended living room. When the hard clay is swept clean as a floor and the fine sand around the edges lined with tiny, irregular grooves, anyone can come and sit and look up into the elm tree and wait for the breezes that never come inside the house.

Maggie will be nervous until after her sister goes: she will stand hopelessly in corners, homely and ashamed of the burn scars down her arms and legs, eying her sister with a mixture of envy and awe. She thinks her sister has held life always in the palm of one hand, that "no" is a word the world never learned to say to her.

* * *

You've no doubt seen those TV shows where the child who has "made it" is confronted, as a surprise, by her own mother and father, tottering in weakly from backstage. (A pleasant surprise, of course: What would they do if parent and child came on the show only to curse out and insult each other?) On TV mother and child embrace and smile into each other's faces. Sometimes the mother and father weep, the child wraps them in her arms and leans across the table to tell how she would not have made it without their help. I have seen these programs.

Sometimes I dream a dream in which Dee and I are suddenly brought together on a TV program of this sort. Out of a dark and soft-seated limousine I am ushered into a bright room filled with many people. There I meet a smiling, gray, sporty man like Johnny Carson who shakes my hand and tells me what a fine girl I have. Then we are on the stage and Dee is embracing me with tears in her eyes. She pins on my dress a large orchid, even though she has told me once that she thinks orchids are tacky flowers.

In real life I am a large, big-boned woman with rough, man-working hands. In the winter I wear flannel nightgowns to bed and overalls during the day. I can kill and clean a hog as mercilessly as a man. My fat keeps me hot in zero weather. I can work outside all day, breaking ice to get water for washing; I can eat pork liver cooked over the open fire minutes after it comes steaming from the hog. One winter I knocked a bull calf straight in the brain between the eyes with a sledge hammer and had the meat hung up to chill before nightfall. But of course all this does not show on television. I am the way my daughter would want me to be: a hundred pounds lighter, my skin like an uncooked barley pancake. My hair glistens in the hot bright lights. Johnny Carson has much to do to keep up with my quick and witty tongue.

But that is a mistake. I know even before I wake up. Who ever knew a Johnson with a quick tongue? Who can even imagine me looking a strange white man in the eye? It seems to me I have talked to them always with one foot raised in flight, with my head turned in whichever way is farthest from them. Dee, though. She would always look anyone in the eye. Hesitation was no part of her nature.

"How do I look, Mama?" Maggie says, showing just enough of her thin body enveloped in pink skirt and red blouse for me to know she's there, almost hidden by the door.

"Come out into the yard," I say.

Have you ever seen a lame animal, perhaps a dog run over by some careless person rich enough to own a car, sidle up to someone who is ignorant enough to be kind to him? That is the way my Maggie walks. She has been like this, chin on chest, eyes on ground, feet in shuffle, ever since the fire that burned the other house to the ground.

Dee is lighter than Maggie, with nicer hair and a fuller figure. She's a woman now, though sometimes I forget. How long ago was it that the other house burned? Ten, twelve years? Sometimes I can still hear the flames and feel Maggie's arms sticking to me, her hair smoking and her dress falling off her in little black papery flakes. Her eyes seemed stretched open, blazed open by the flames reflected in them. And Dee. I see her standing off under the sweet gum tree she used to dig gum out of; a look of concentration on her face as she watched the last dingy gray board of the house fall in toward the red-hot brick chimney. Why don't you do a dance around the ashes? I'd wanted to ask her. She had hated the house that much.

I used to think she hated Maggie, too. But that was before we raised the money, the church and me, to send her to Augusta to school. She used to read to us without pity; forcing words, lies, other folks' habits, whole lives upon us two, sitting trapped and ignorant underneath her voice. She washed us in a river of make-believe, burned us with a lot of knowledge we didn't necessarily need to know. Pressed us to her with the serious way she read, to shove us away at just the moment, like dimwits, we seemed about to understand.

Dee wanted nice things. A yellow organdy dress to wear to her graduation from high school; black pumps to match a green suit she'd made from an old suit somebody gave me. She was determined to stare down any disaster in her efforts. Her eyelids would not flicker for minutes at a time. Often I fought off the temptation to shake her. At sixteen she had a style of her own: and knew what style was.

I never had an education myself. After second grade the school was closed down. Don't ask me why: in 1927 colored asked fewer questions than they do now. Sometimes Maggie reads to me. She stumbles along good-naturedly but can't see well. She knows she is not bright. Like good looks and money, quickness passed her by. She will marry John Thomas (who has mossy teeth in an earnest face) and then I'll be free to sit here and I guess just sing church songs to myself. Although I never was a good singer. Never could carry a tune. I was always better at a man's job. I used to love to milk till I was hooked in the side in '49. Cows are soothing and slow and don't bother you, unless you try to milk them the wrong way.

I have deliberately turned my back on the house. It is three rooms, just like the one that burned, except the roof is tin; they don't make shingle roofs any more. There are no real windows, just some holes cut in the sides, like the portholes in a ship, but not round and not square, with rawhide holding the shutters up on the outside. This house is in a pasture, too, like the other one. No doubt when Dee sees it she will want to tear it down. She wrote me once that no matter where we "choose" to live, she will manage to come see us. But she will never bring her friends. Maggie and I thought about this and Maggie asked me, "Mama, when did Dee ever *have* any friends?"

She had a few. Furtive boys in pink shirts hanging about on washday after school. Nervous girls who never laughed. Impressed with her they worshiped the well-turned phrase, the cute shape, the scalding humor that erupted like bubbles in lye. She read to them.

When she was courting Jimmy T she didn't have much time to pay to us, but turned all her faultfinding power on him. He *flew* to marry a cheap city girl from a family of ignorant flashy people. She hardly had time to recompose herself.

When she comes I will meet—but there they are!

Maggie attempts to make a dash for the house, in her shuffling way, but I stay her with my hand. "Come back here," I say. And she stops and tries to dig a well in the sand with her toe.

It is hard to see them clearly through the strong sun. But even the first glimpse of leg out of the car tells me it is Dee. Her feet were always neat-looking, as if God himself had shaped them with a certain style. From the other side of the car comes a short, stocky man. Hair is all over his head a foot long and hanging from his chin like a kinky mule tail. I hear Maggie suck in her breath. "Uhnnnh," is what it sounds like. Like when you see the wriggling end of a snake just in front of your foot on the road. "Uhnnnh."

Dee next. A dress down to the ground, in this hot weather. A dress so loud it hurts my eyes. There are yellows and oranges enough to throw back the light of the sun. I feel my whole face warming from the heat waves it throws out. Earrings gold, too, and hanging down to her shoulders. Bracelets dangling and making noises when she moves her arm up to shake the folds of the dress out of her armpits. The dress is loose and flows, and as she walks closer, I like it. I hear Maggie go "Uhnnnh" again. It is her sister's hair. It stands straight up like the wool on a sheep. It is black as night and around the edges are two long pigtails that rope about like small lizards disappearing behind her ears.

"Wa-su-zo-Tean-o!" she says, coming on in that gliding way the dress makes her move. The short stocky fellow with the hair to his navel is all grinning and he follows up with "Asalamalakim, my mother and sister!" He moves to hug Maggie but she falls back, right up against the back of my chair. I feel her trembling there and when I look up I see the perspiration falling off her chin.

"Don't get up," says Dee. Since I am stout it takes something of a push. You can see me trying to move a second or two before I make it. She turns, showing white heels through her sandals, and goes back to the car. Out she peeks next with a Polaroid. She stoops down quickly and lines up picture after picture of me sitting there in front of the house with Maggie cowering behind me. She never takes a shot without making sure the house is included. When a cow comes nibbling around the edge of the yard she snaps it and me and Maggie *and* the house. Then she puts the Polaroid in the back seat of the car, and comes up and kisses me on the forehead.

Meanwhile Asalamalakim is going through motions with Maggie's hand. Maggie's hand is as limp as a fish, and probably as cold, despite the sweat, and she keeps trying to pull it back. It looks like Asalamalakim wants to shake hands but wants to do it fancy. Or maybe he don't know how people shake hands. Anyhow, he soon gives up on Maggie.

"Well," I say. "Dee."

"No, Mama," she says. "Not 'Dee,' Wangero Leewanika Kemanjo!"

"What happened to 'Dee'?" I wanted to know.

"She's dead," Wangero said. "I couldn't bear it any longer, being named after the people who oppress me."

"You know as well as me you was named after your aunt Dicie," I said. Dicie is my sister. She named Dee. We called her "Big Dee" after Dee was born.

"But who was *she* named after?" asked Wangero.

"I guess after Grandma Dee," I said.

"And who was she named after?" asked Wangero.

"Her mother," I said, and saw Wangero was getting tired. "That's about as far back as I can trace it," I said. Though, in fact, I probably could have carried it back beyond the Civil War through the branches.

"Well," said Asalamalakim, "there you are."

"Uhnnnh," I heard Maggie say.

"There I was not," I said, "before 'Dicie' cropped up in our family, so why should I try to trace it that far back?"

He just stood there grinning, looking down on me like somebody inspecting a Model A car. Every once in a while he and Wangero sent eye signals over my head.

"How do you pronounce this name?" I asked.

"You don't have to call me by it if you don't want to," said Wangero.

"Why shouldn't I?" I asked. "If that's what you want us to call you, we'll call you."

"I know it might sound awkward at first," said Wangero.

"I'll get used to it," I said. "Ream it out again."

Well, soon we got the name out of the way. Asalamalakim had a name twice as long and three times as hard. After I tripped over it two or three times he told me to just call him Hakim-a-barber. I wanted to ask him was he a barber, but I didn't really think he was, so I didn't ask.

"You must belong to those beef-cattle peoples down the road," I said. They said "Asalamalakim" when they met you, too, but they didn't shake hands. Always too busy: feeding the cattle, fixing the fences, putting up salt-lick shelters, throwing down hay. When the white folks poisoned some of the herd the men stayed up all night with rifles in their hands. I walked a mile and a half just to see the sight.

Hakim-a-barber said, "I accept some of their doctrines, but farming and raising cattle is not my style." (They didn't tell me, and I didn't ask, whether Wangero (Dee) had really gone and married him.)

We sat down to eat and right away he said he didn't eat collards and pork was unclean. Wangero, though, went on through the chitlins and corn bread, the greens and everything else. She talked a blue streak over the sweet potatoes. Everything delighted her. Even the fact that we still used the benches her daddy made for the table when we couldn't afford to buy chairs.

"Oh, Mama!" she cried. Then turned to Hakim-a-barber. "I never knew how lovely these benches are. You can feel the rump prints," she said, running her hands underneath her and along the bench. Then she gave a sigh and her hand closed over Grandma Dee's butter dish. "That's it!" she said. "I knew there was something I wanted to ask you if I could have." She jumped up from the table and went over in the corner where the churn stood, the milk in it clabber by now. She looked at the churn and looked at it.

"This churn top is what I need," she said. "Didn't Uncle Buddy whittle it out of a tree you all used to have?"

"Yes," I said.

"Uh huh," she said happily. "And I want the dasher, too."

"Uncle Buddy whittle that, too?" asked the barber.

Dee (Wangero) looked up at me.

"Aunt Dee's first husband whittled the dash," said Maggie so low you almost couldn't hear her. "His name was Henry, but they called him Stash."

"Maggie's brain is like an elephant's," Wangero said, laughing. "I can use the churn top as a centerpiece for the alcove table," she said, sliding a plate over the churn, "and I'll think of something artistic to do with the dasher."

When she finished wrapping the dasher the handle stuck out. I took it for a moment in my hands. You didn't even have to look close to see where hands pushing the dasher up and down to make butter had left a kind of sink in the wood. In fact, there were a lot of small sinks; you could see where thumbs and fingers had sunk into the wood. It was beautiful light yellow wood, from a tree that grew in the yard where Big Dee and Stash had lived.

After dinner Dee (Wangero) went to the trunk at the

foot of my bed and started rifling through it. Maggie hung back in the kitchen over the dishpan. Out came Wangero with two quilts. They had been pieced by Grandma Dee and then Big Dee and me had hung them on the quilt frames on the front porch and quilted them. One was in the Lone Star pattern. The other was Walk Around the Mountain. In both of them were scraps of dresses Grandma Dee had worn fifty and more years ago. Bits and pieces of Grandpa Jarrell's paisley shirts. And one teeny faded blue piece, about the size of a penny matchbox, that was from Great Grandpa Ezra's uniform that he wore in the Civil War.

"Mama," Wangero said sweet as a bird. "Can I have these old quilts?"

I heard something fall in the kitchen, and a minute later the kitchen door slammed.

"Why don't you take one or two of the others?" I asked. "These old things was just done by me and Big Dee from some tops your grandma pieced before she died."

"No," said Wangero. "I don't want those. They are stitched around the borders by machine."

"That'll make them last better," I said.

"That's not the point," said Wangero. "These are all pieces of dresses Grandma used to wear. She did all this stitching by hand. Imagine!" She held the quilts securely in her arms, stroking them.

"Some of the pieces, like those lavender ones, come from old clothes her mother handed down to her," I said, moving up to touch the quilts. Dee (Wangero) moved back just enough so that I couldn't reach the quilts. They already belonged to her.

"Imagine!" she breathed again, clutching them closely to her bosom.

"The truth is," I said, "I promised to give them quilts to Maggie, for when she marries John Thomas."

She gasped like a bee had stung her.

"Maggie can't appreciate these quilts!" she said. "She'd probably be backward enough to put them to everyday use."

"I reckon she would," I said. "God knows I been saving 'em for long enough with nobody using 'em. I hope she will!" I didn't want to bring up how I had offered Dee (Wangero) a quilt when she went away to college. Then she had told me they were old-fashioned, out of style.

"But they're *priceless!*" she was saying now, furiously; for she has a temper. "Maggie would put them on the bed and in five years they'd be in rags. Less than that!" "She can always make some more," I said. "Maggie knows how to quilt."

Dee (Wangero) looked at me with hatred. "You just will not understand. The point is these quilts, *these* quilts!"

"Well," I said, stumped. "What would *you* do with them?"

"Hang them," she said. As if that was the only thing you *could* do with quilts.

Maggie by now was standing in the door. I could almost hear the sound her feet made as they scraped over each other.

"She can have them, Mama," she said, like somebody used to never winning anything, or having anything reserved for her. "I can 'member Grandma Dee without the quilts."

I looked at her hard. She had filled her bottom lip with checkerberry snuff and it gave her face a kind of dopey, hang-dog look. It was Grandma Dee and Big Dee who taught her how to quilt herself. She stood there with her scarred hands hidden in the folds of her skirt. She looked at her sister with something like fear but she wasn't mad at her. This was Maggie's portion. This was the way she knew God to work.

When I looked at her like that something hit me in the top of my head and ran down to the soles of my feet. Just like when I'm in church and the spirit of God touches me and I get happy and shout. I did something I never had done before: hugged Maggie to me, then dragged her on into the room, snatched the quilts out of Miss Wangero's hands and dumped them into Maggie's lap. Maggie just sat there on my bed with her mouth open.

"Take one or two of the others," I said to Dee.

But she turned without a word and went out to Hakim-a-barber.

"You just don't understand," she said, as Maggie and I came out to the car.

"What don't I understand?" I wanted to know.

"Your heritage," she said. And then she turned to Maggie, kissed her, and said, "You ought to try to make something of yourself, too, Maggie. It's really a new day for us. But from the way you and Mama still live you'd never know it."

She put on some sunglasses that hid everything above the tip of her nose and her chin.

Maggie smiled; maybe at the sunglasses. But a real smile, not scared. After we watched the car dust settle I asked Maggie to bring me a dip of snuff. And then the two of us sat there just enjoying, until it was time to go in the house and go to bed.

Groom Service

Michael Dorris

"She's a piece of pure agate," Bernard's mother Martha said to Marie's mother Blanche. "A one in a million that you find after walking the beach for half your life with your eyes on the ground. If I had a child like that I would keep her in a safe place."

Blanche paused, her blade midway down the side of the fish she was scaling. Her face betrayed no expression except exertion, and even in this intermission her teeth remained set against each other, flexing her jaw. The trader steel reflected what little light filtered through the planks of the smokehouse, and the confined air still smelled green. Blanche had hewn the boards with a mallet and chisel in May, as soon as the ground firmed from the spring runoff, and it took a while before the scent of fire crowded that of drying wood. With her broad thumb she flicked a piece of fin off the carved knife handle, then continued her motion.

Martha waited. She had all the time it took.

"You don't know," said Blanche. She shook her head as if its secrets rolled like line weights from side to side. She drew a heavy breath. "You can't imagine. You with such a boy."

Martha sat straighter, all ears, while her hands continued to explore, repairing the tears on the net that lay across her lap and hid her pants and boots. Her fingers moved automatically, finding holes, locating the ends of broken cord and twisting them into bow knots. She kept her nails sharp and jagged, and when they weren't enough she bowed her head and bit off any useless pieces. This was mindless work, the labor of ten thousand days, and could be done as easily in the dark as in the light. It required no involvement. Her thoughts were elsewhere.

"You mean Bernard?" Her voice was wary. She had three sons and needed to be sure she knew the one Blanche had in mind.

"Ber-*nard*," Blanche nodded, giving the knife a last run, then inspecting the fish closely before tossing it into the large basket at her feet. The water slopped onto the floor and, from there, leaked to the shale ground inches below. Blanche arched her back and massaged her spine with her fist. With her other hand she reached for the cup of cooled tea that she had nursed for the past half hour. Martha let the net rest and joined her.

"People talk about him, you know," Blanche said. "His looks, that goes without saying, but the other things too. The respect he pays the old folks. His singing. His calmness. His hunting skill. You must be proud."

Martha closed her eyes as if in great pain. "He is my punishment," she confessed, "but I don't know what I could have done so terrible as to deserve him. He stays out till all hours. His hair is always tangled. I sometimes think that the game he brings home has died before he found it, the meat is so tough. You must have him confused with another boy. Or perhaps, with a girl like Marie, you find it hard to think ill of any child."

"Now you make fun of me," Blanche said. "It is well known that Marie has turned out badly. She is lazy and disrespectful, conceited and stubborn. I try my best to teach her, and so do my sisters and even my mother, but she folds her arms and stares at nothing. Hopeless. And she will never find a husband. A boy's mother would have to be desperate to send her son courting at my house."

"But not as desperate as the mother who could tolerate the thought of Bernard as a son-in-law," Martha said. "That would be true desperation. I will never be free of him. I will grow old with him at my side, and with no granddaughters or grandsons to comfort me."

"If only someone like your Bernard would find an interest in Marie," Blanche said as if she had not heard Martha. "If only some young man exactly like him would consent to live in my house, how I would welcome him. I would treat him as my own blood."

The two women met each other's gaze at last. Each raised a cup to her lips, and after a few seconds, each drank. Each replaced her cup on the table between them. Each held her mouth firm. Blanche found her knife and reached for a new fish, cool and slippery as a stone over which much water has rushed. Martha shifted the net in her lap, moving a new section to the center. The smell of salt rose like steam as her hands went to work.

"I will speak to him," Martha said.

"And I to her," Blanche replied. "But I know her answer already. I have seen how she regards him."

"She will not be disappointed." Martha allowed one wave of pride to crest. "He's not so bad."

Blanche glanced at Martha, then looked quickly back to her work. Bernard must be good indeed, she thought, if Martha could not better contain herself.

II.

Bernard was drawing with charcoal on a piece of driftwood when his mother returned home. He was twenty-two, lean, and had large teeth. His eyes were dark beneath unusually thick brows, and his hands were long and broad. At the sound of Martha's step, he jumped to his feet and assumed the air of a person about to do something important. His fingers curved as if to hold a tool or a weapon and his eyes narrowed as if to see something far away. He was busy at nothing, his energy humming, ready for a focus. But for once she made no comment about his sloth. She did not despair at the time he wasted scratching on any smooth surface. She did not inspect his sketch and then toss it into the cooking fire. In fact, this afternoon she regarded him rather mildly.

"Well, it's arranged," she announced. "I spent an endless morning with your future mother-in-law and before I left she had agreed to let you come to see Marie. Don't think it was easy."

Bernard's eyes followed his mother's movements as she crossed the floor and sat in exhaustion on the bed. She pushed off her boots, still caked with beach mud, and rubbed her feet together. She wore no socks.

"Marie?" he said at last. "She's too young. You should have asked me first."

Martha's glare clapped a hand over his mouth. In a moment, Bernard tried again.

"I know they're a good family. I know you want to do right for me. But you could . . . we could have discussed this. I mean, I think of her as a little girl, not a *wife.*" The word, a stranger to Bernard's vocabulary, vibrated in the air.

"Stop whining," Martha said, losing patience. "Who do you 'think of' as a wife? *Doris?*"

Bernard blushed. He wasn't surprised that his mother knew about him and Doris, but it did not seem fair for her to mention it. Doris was a widow whose name brought nervous laughs to teen-age boys and frowns of disapproval to everyone else. She was a woman almost twice Bernard's age with a missing front tooth and eyes that sparked in his memory, a woman who had summoned him for an errand six months ago and whom he now loved better than he would have thought possible, and not just for the way she moved. But it was true: he had never thought of Doris as a wife.

"You should see yourself," Martha said. "Keep that face and you won't have to worry about marrying anyone. But don't expect me to support you forever." She noticed the driftwood, still on the floor, and nudged it with her toe to get a better look. Bernard had outlined the mountain across the bay from the village, and tucked a large sun behind its peak. When he drew it he thought it was his best work, but now its lines looked smudged and shaky. Martha leaned forward to pick it up and turn it over, as if expecting another illustration on the back. Finding none, she held it out for Bernard to take.

"Give this to your Doris," she said. "It looks like her under the blanket where she spends her time."

Bernard didn't move, but he watched the wood until his mother let it fall to the floor. He was angry at the shame he felt. He was angry that he knew it was just a matter of time until he would have to call on Marie. He was angry that his mother was right: his mountain *did* look like Doris, turned on her side.

III.

When Blanche went into the house and told Marie that their problems were over, that Bernard, the catch of the village, would be courting, she expected some reaction, but her daughter simply folded her arms and stared at nothing.

"Don't you hear me?" Blanche demanded. "Bernard. Coming to see you. Can't you be happy? Can't you say something?"

Marie, however, only rolled her eyes and drummed her fingers against the bench upon which she sat. She wore a closeknit woven cap that, in combination with her unfortunately weak chin, made her head resemble an acorn. She was fifteen, just out of her confinement, trained for adulthood to the limits of Blanche and her sisters' abilities, but still a sulking child. At length she drew up her knees, circled them with her arms, and watched her mother from the corner of her eye.

Blanche was across the long room, talking to her older sister Bonnie. She was not hard to overhear.

"Does she say 'thank you'? Does she appreciate what it means to her, to all of us, to get that damn Martha to agree? Does she care that Bernard could have any girl, from any family?"

Bonnie shook her head sadly. Her surviving children had all been boys and had long since moved to the houses of their wives' families, so she had no experience with reluctant girls, unless, she thought, she counted her memories of Blanche. But that would not do to say, especially not in earshot of Marie, who sat with her head cocked in their direction. Blanche's daughter was the hope of the next generation, the one who had to bring in a husband and produce more daughters than her mother or aunt, if the family was to regain its position. For a moment Bonnie thought of suggesting to Blanche that they present that information to Marie directly, to drop the shadows and point out both her responsibility and her power, but then she rejected the idea. The girl was impressed enough with herself as it was. Instead, Bonnie sympathized with her sister and cast occasional looks at her niece in hopes of catching on Marie's face a secret, fleeting expression of pleasure.

IV.

"What am I supposed to do?" Bernard asked the next time his uncle visited. Bernard had waited for a private moment, and it came when, just before sleep, Theodore had stepped outside to relieve himself.

From the darkness came rattling sounds of strangulation that Bernard eventually identified as the older man's yawn. When it, and the noise of splashing water, had abated, Theodore spoke. It was clear that he understood Bernard's problem.

"You do whatever they tell you and you hope they're not as bad as they could be," Theodore said. "You don't complain. You don't assume anything. You stay out of the way, because you never know what they're going to find to dislike. You be what they want."

"It's not fair." Bernard leaned against the side of the house and searched the sky. Thin clouds, silver as wet spider webs, passed in the night wind.

"That's true, but there are other things in the world besides owning real estate. Your true home will remain here in your mother's house, just as it has been for me, but you can't *live* here forever. You need independence, distance, the chance to be a man in a place where you were never a boy. Once you get yourself established, once you pay your dues, you'll understand what I mean. Your life is not all indoors. You'll hang around with your brothers-in-law, your uncles, your friends. Spend time at the men's club. Go to the sweat bath and gripe, or listen to the complaints of others and make jokes. In a year all your wife's family will care about is whether or not you bring in your share. By then you'll know what's what."

"But what if I don't get along with Marie?"

"*Do* get along with her. Get along with her mother. Get along with her auntie. But on your own time do what you want. It's not a big price to pay. It's a daughter-poor clan and the one they've picked out for you is going to control everything someday: fabulous fishing sights, a big house. Behave yourself now and you'll get your reward. It's not like you're marrying a youngest sister with no prospects."

Which was, Bernard knew, what had happened to Theodore. No wonder he was not more sympathetic.

"How do I tell Doris?" Bernard asked. This was something he had struggled with for days.

"Doris! She could have told you. It's good news to her. She gets a younger guy, fresh the way she likes them, and no hard feelings between you." Theodore laughed, not unkindly, and put an arm around Bernard's shoulders. "Listen to some advice, from your great-uncle through me to you," he said. "The groom service is the worst part, so make it as short as possible by winning over her family. Convince them you won't be a pain in the ass to live with. And to do that, rule number one is, whatever you do, be appreciative. Fall all over yourself."

"Did you do that?" Bernard asked. "Did my mother's husband do that?"

"Do fish swim underwater? But don't take my word for it. Ask Pete. He's your father."

"I'd be embarrassed," Bernard said. "He and I never talk about serious matters, and this is not the kind of thing you can easily ask a person who's not of the clan."

"It's every man for himself, when it comes right down to it," Theodore said. "Let's go in. You're going to need sleep."

V.

"This is what you do," Martha instructed.

It was not yet light and she had awakened Bernard

from a sound sleep. He blew into a cup of hot tea as he listened, letting the darkness hide the resentment in his face.

"You go hunting and you catch something *good,* I don't care what. Something a little unusual. A beaver, maybe, or a goose. *Not* something small and easy. *Not* a squirrel. *Not* fish. You bring it home and I'll help you clean it. You leave a portion for me as if that's what you always do, to help provide for your family, but you take the best part with you and you park yourself in front of Blanche's door. You only speak if you're spoken to. You wait for *them* to ask *you.* And if they don't, which they won't right away, you act unconcerned. You do this every day until they invite you in, and then I'll tell you what to do next. This is your chance, so don't ruin it. Now move."

Bernard stepped out into the chill morning grayness, thought briefly of visiting Doris before he went hunting, but then abandoned the idea. He had heard through his mother's husband that Doris had made friends with a seventeen-year-old boy named James.

The dew from high grass had soaked through to Bernard's feet before he reached the edge of the woods. He realized his mother had forgotten to feed him breakfast, forgotten to make him a lunch. He heard a duck call from the lake and paused, but then continued on. He could hear his mother in his mind, and she said a duck wouldn't do.

VI.

"He's *there!*" Bonnie dropped the firewood she was carrying and rushed to Blanche's side.

Her sister was stirring a pot on the fire, a study in indifference. "I have eyes," Blanche said. "Keep your voice down. He'll hear you."

"Did you see what he had?" Bonnie asked. "I got a glimpse of something brown but I didn't want him to catch me looking."

"I think it was a beaver. Or an otter. Would you believe, he had the nerve to hold it up to me and smile the first time I passed."

"No!"

"I thought he was better trained. It simply means he'll have to wait longer."

"Did Marie see him yet?"

"She won't go out the door." Both sisters turned to the gloom in the rear of the room where Marie crouched, her head lowered over a stick game. Her long hair was loose and covered her shoulders like a shawl.

"She *could* try to fix herself up a bit," Blanche said, loud enough to be heard.

"Give her time," Bonnie whispered. "She's young."

VII.

"Well, what happened?" Martha demanded when Bernard returned home late in the evening.

"Nothing happened," Bernard said, and threw himself down on his blankets. He raised an arm to cover his eyes, then turned to face the wall.

Martha spotted the sack her son had dropped on the floor and looked inside. The beaver tail and quarters were exactly as she had cleaned them that afternoon, and she took them out to add to the broth she had prepared.

"At least we'll eat well for a while," she said.

"I'm not hungry," Bernard replied, but his mother ignored him.

"Tell me everything."

"There's nothing to tell. I walked over there, dressed like I was going to a party, carrying that beaver. I never caught such a one. I surprised it so there wasn't even adrenaline in its blood. I thought they'd see it and invite me to supper, but they walked by me like I wasn't there, their noses in the air."

"Whose noses?" Martha wanted to know.

"The mother and the aunt."

"Not the girl?"

"I saw no girl. I heard no girl."

"Ah," said Martha. "So she's shy. Good."

"Why good?"

"Because then she won't bully you at first, stupid boy. I've seen what happens to the husbands of the bold ones."

The smell of stewing meat filled the room, warm, rich, brown. Martha's husband Pete came into the house at the scent, tipped his head in his son's direction, and asked, "Hard day?"

VIII.

For a week, then two weeks, the same pattern was repeated. Only the animals changed: they ranged from a porcupine to a hind quarter of caribou, from a fat grouse on a bad day to a string of matched silver salmon on a good one. Once Bernard thought he saw a black bear dive into the brush at the side of a stream, but he was momentarily afraid to investigate, and later berated himself. With a bearskin, he thought too late, he would have been irresistible and his long afternoons and evenings at Blanche's closed door would have been over.

As a month passed, Bernard lost hope. He lost the alertness he had once felt when Blanche or Bonnie or Marie, the most unsympathetic of them all, approached, and he soon tired of the commiseration that Blanche's and Bonnie's husbands cast in his direction as they went about their business. They could remember, their expressions said, what it was like to wait outside this house, but there was nothing they could do. A word from them might slow the process rather than speed it up, might do more harm than good. If boredom was patience, Bernard achieved patience. If learning to exist without expectation of fulfillment was maturity, Bernard matured. At first he used his time to remember Doris, to wonder what she was doing and to regret not doing it with her. Later he thought about hunting, how he could have succeeded the times he had failed, how the animals behaved, how they smelled and sounded. Finally he found himself thinking about Pete, his father, in different ways than he ever had before. In Bernard's mind Pete became more than just his father, more than just his mother's husband; he became another man, an earlier version of Bernard, a fellow sufferer. It had not previously occurred to Bernard how hard it was to be forever a stranger in the house where you lived, to be always a half visitor. He wondered how Pete stayed so cheerful, and wondered if Martha's mother had kept his father waiting long at her door before inviting him inside. On an afternoon late in the second week, Bernard had a thought so profound, so unprecedented, that it startled him into erect posture. What if, he wondered, his grandmother had not let Pete in at all? What if Pete had been judged inadequate? Where would that have left Bernard?

The next morning when he went hunting Bernard returned to the place where he had seen the bear, hid himself behind a log, and waited.

IX.

"Did you hear?" Pete asked Theodore as they walked the trail from the steam bath to their wives' houses.

"About Bernard's bear?"

"It must have weighed three hundred pounds. I didn't know Bernard had it in him."

"Have you forgotten what sitting in front of a house will drive you to? What did you catch to get inside Martha's?"

"Nothing," Pete said. "It was me she couldn't resist."

"You forget," Theodore replied. "I was still a boy in that house. I recall their words of you. Let me see . . . I seem to remember some mention of the small size of certain of your parts."

"Poor brother-in-law," Pete said. "You still don't realize the lengths to which they went to avoid hurting your feelings! And how *is* your wife? How is the health of her many elder sisters? Is it true that they become stronger and more robust with every year?"

X.

On the second day of the fifth week, just as she passed through the door, Blanche reached down her right hand and snagged one of the bear claws that rested in the basket by Bernard's leg. So quick was her movement, so apparently disconnected to the business on her mind, so complete her distraction, that Bernard had to look twice to make sure it was gone. All the same, he felt a warm flush spread beneath the skin of his neck, and a feeling of inordinate pride suffused him so thoroughly that he had difficulty remaining still. He had been found worthy, and now it was only a matter of time.

Every day now, and each time with more pause and deliberation, Blanche browsed through his offerings and always selected some prize. Her expression betrayed no gratitude, yet Bernard was sure that occasionally she was pleasantly surprised. Afraid to unbalance their precarious arrangement, he sat still as a listening hare in her presence, not even a bystander at her shopping. He kept his eyes lowered and held his breath until she had departed, but remained ever watchful for any cue that the situation had progressed to another stage. At last it came.

"Bernard!" Blanche said one day, looking out the door. "Is that you crouching there so quietly? Please, come in and share our supper, poor as it is. What a pleasure to see you."

Bernard rose slowly, stiff in his joints and half skeptical that this was some joke, some new test, but when he entered the house Blanche's hospitality continued and was joined by that of Bonnie, who sat by the fire trimming her husband's hair with a squeaking scissors. "Sit, sit." She motioned to a bench near the door. "What a shy boy you are. Luckily we have some nice moose to feed you."

Indeed they did. Bernard recognized the remains of the foreleg he had offered yesterday. Bonnie passed him a plate with a small portion of tough gristle, gray and cooled. He knew what to say.

"This is wonderful," he exclaimed. "The best I've ever

tasted. What cooks you are. But you are too generous. Let me put some back in the pot."

When they refused, politely and with many denials of his compliments, Bernard made a great show of eating. The act of digestion absorbed his total concentration. He rubbed his stomach and cast his eyes to the ceiling in delight. With great subtlety he periodically raised his hand to his mouth, as if to wipe some grease, and used that motion to conceal the small bits of undigestible food he removed from his cheeks and tucked secretly into his pockets.

When he finished, Bernard sat nervously, breathless with anxiety. From the corner of his eye he detected a space so devoid of movement that it attracted his attention. He looked, then quickly looked away. Yet his eyes still registered the image of Marie, her hair oiled and braided, wearing a new dress and a necklace made of bear claws, sitting composed and shaded as a perfect charcoal sketch. He thought she was truly beautiful.

XI.

"You know, Pete," Martha said as she lay by her husband's side under a blanket, "watching Bernard lately brings back memories."

"To me too. Your mother was a terror."

"I notice you still whisper such words, even though she's more than four years gone."

Pete shifted his position and propped on an elbow. In the moonlight Martha's face looked seamless and young. A beam like the hottest part of a coal danced off her dark eye. He ran his fingers along her cheek and she turned her head in comfort. "You look the same as then," he said.

Martha caught his hand and brought it to her mouth, let it feel the smile.

"I pestered her, you know, to let you in," she said. "You didn't know I was alive."

"I didn't know the day you found the eagle feathers? I didn't know the day you came an hour later than always?"

"It was raining," Pete said. "The ground was soft and I kept sinking to my knees. I couldn't arrive at your door covered in mud."

"I thought you weren't coming. I confronted my mother and told her that her slowness had cost me . . ."

"Cost you what?" Pete asked, when Martha's silence persisted.

"Enough talk."

XII.

Marie watched the back of Bernard's head and admired the dark sheen of his long hair, the play of muscles in his arms at his every movement. During the last month she had studied every part of him so completely that she could create him in her imagination whenever she chose, and lately, she chose often. She had to fight not to laugh when they gave him the worst meat and he had to spit into his hand and act as though it were delicious. She watched the way his fingers held the plate, the way he sat so compact and attentive. She waited for the sound of his soft voice and wondered what he would say when he could speak in private. She made a game of observing his eyes until just the second before they turned to her, and believed she had been discovered only once.

XIII.

Bernard ate almost all of his meals at Blanche's house now, and gradually had become more relaxed. For one thing, his distribution increased in both quality and quantity, and he could now expect a reasonably digestible piece of meat or salmon. For another, Blanche and Bonnie's husbands had begun to join him on his hunts, to show him places to fish that only the members of this household knew. He found he liked these men and began to call them "uncle."

Blanche herself still frightened him, but not all the time. There were moments when he found approval in her gaze, times when some word of hers sounded almost like a joke. Bonnie was warmer, more solicitous of his needs, more complimentary of the food he brought, and Bernard thought of her as an ally.

As far as Marie was concerned, he still had no clue to her feelings. Even Pete and Theodore observed that this game was lasting longer than the usual and debated whether something might be wrong. They were full of advice for Bernard, full of ideas of how to please Marie, full of reminders that it was her agreement, in the last analysis, which was necessary. But no matter what Bernard did, Marie would not look at him or give him any sign of encouragement. He grew despondent, lost his appetite, found himself thinking once again of Doris and the ease of their association. Marie seemed totally beyond his reach, the focus of mystery and impossible desire. And so he was unprepared on the night, just before the first frost of winter, when, with shaking hands, Marie herself passed him a plate of food.

"This is for you," she said so softly he could barely hear, and she sat beside him while, slowly and with great emotion, he ate.

XIV.

A year later, while waiting for the birth of Marie's first child, Blanche and Martha passed the time by nibbling strips of dried eel. Martha, who had no love for the oily skin, threw hers into the fire, where it sizzled briefly.

"The midwife predicts a girl," Blanche said. "When she spun the charm above Marie's stomach, it revolved to the left."

"A girl is most rewarding," Martha nodded. "But there is a special satisfaction in raising boys. So often I think of times when Bernard was young, so often I miss him around the house."

Blanche reached for another stick of *baleek* and did not answer. Her silence was immediately noticed, as she knew it would be.

"How is he doing?" Martha asked at last.

"He will learn," Blanche said. "He has potential. It is clear he cares greatly for Marie, and she is patient."

"That is one word for it." Martha tossed a handful of scraps into the flame and watched the light flare and dance. "Of course Bernard was used to . . . He had such a *happy* home that I'm sure it has taken some adjusting on his part in new surroundings."

"Yes, he was somewhat spoiled. But I think he has a good heart."

"As well he must, to remain loyal to such a chinless girl."

"One only hopes their child will inherit the mother's disposition and not be sulky and resentful of every request."

"One can but pray it will have the father's looks and personality."

A single rope of eel remained on the plate. Both women extended a hand toward it, hesitated, and withdrew. It rested between them as they cleaned their teeth with fine bone picks and slowly wiped the grease from their fingers, and when, at the sound of Marie's first muffled protest, they rose together and rushed to her side, it remained behind.

Fenstad's Mother

Charles Baxter

On Sunday morning after communion Fenstad drove across town to visit his mother. Behind the wheel, he exhaled with his hand flat in front of his mouth to determine if the wine on his breath could be detected. He didn't think so. Fenstad's mother was a lifelong social progressive who was amused by her son's churchgoing, and, wine or no wine, she could guess where he had been. She had spent her life in the company of rebels and deviationists, and she recognized all their styles.

Passing a frozen pond in the city park, Fenstad slowed down to watch the skaters, many of whom he knew by name and skating style. From a distance they were dots of color ready for flight, frictionless. To express grief on skates seemed almost impossible, and Fenstad liked that. He parked his car on a residential block and took out his skates from the back seat, where he kept them all winter. With his fingertips he touched the wooden blade guards, thinking of the time. He checked his watch; he had fifteen minutes.

Out on the ice, still wearing his churchy Sunday-morning suit, tie, and overcoat, but now circling the outside edge of the pond with his bare hands in his overcoat pockets, Fenstad admired the overcast sky and luxuriated in the brittle cold. He was active and alert in winter but felt sleepy throughout the summer. He passed a little girl in a pink jacket, pushing a tiny chair over the ice. He waved to his friend Ann, an off-duty cop, practicing her twirls. He waved to other friends. Without exception they waved back. As usual, he was impressed by the way skates improved human character.

Twenty minutes later, in the doorway of her apartment, his mother said, "Your cheeks are red." She glanced down at his trousers, damp with melted snow. "You've been skating." She kissed him on the cheek and turned to walk into her living room. "Skating after church? Isn't that some sort of error?"

"It's just happiness," Fenstad said. Quickly he checked her apartment for any signs of memory loss or depression. He found none and immediately felt relief. The apartment smelled of soap and Lysol, the signs of an old woman who wouldn't tolerate nonsense. Out on her coffee table, as usual, were the letters she was writing to her congressman and to political dictators around the globe. Fenstad's mother pleaded for enlightened behavior and berated the dictators for their bad political habits.

She grasped the arm of the sofa and let herself down

slowly. Only then did she smile. "How's your soul, Harry?" she asked. "What's the news?"

He smiled back and smoothed his hair. Martin Luther King's eyes looked into his from the framed picture on the wall opposite him. In the picture King was shaking hands with Fenstad's mother, the two of them surrounded by smiling faces. "My soul's okay, Ma," he said. "It's a hard project. I'm always working on it." He reached down for a chocolate-chunk cookie from a box on top of the television. "Who brought you these?"

"Your daughter Sharon. She came to see me on Friday." Fenstad's mother tilted her head at him. "You *want* to be a good person, but she's the real article. Goodness comes to her without any effort at all. She says you have a new girlfriend. A pharmacist this time. Susan, is it?" Fenstad nodded. "Harry, why does your generation always have to find the right person? Why can't you learn to live with the wrong person? Sooner or later everyone's wrong. Love isn't the most important thing, Harry, far from it. Why can't you see that? I still don't comprehend why you couldn't live with Eleanor." Eleanor was Fenstad's ex-wife. They had been divorced for a decade, but Fenstad's mother hoped for a reconciliation.

"Come on, Ma," Fenstad said. "Over and done with, gone and gone." He took another cookie.

"You live with somebody so that you're living with *somebody,* and then you go out and do the work of the world. I don't understand all this pickiness about lovers. In a pinch anybody'll do, Harry, believe me."

On the side table was a picture of her late husband, Fenstad's mild, middle-of-the-road father. Fenstad glanced at the picture and let the silence hang between them before asking, "How are you, Ma?"

"I'm all right." She leaned back in the sofa, whose springs made a strange, almost human groan. "I want to get out. I spend too much time in this place in January. You should expand my horizons. Take me somewhere."

"Come to my composition class," Fenstad said. "I'll pick you up at dinnertime on Tuesday. Eat early."

"They'll notice me," she said, squinting. "I'm too old."

"I'll introduce you," her son said. "You'll fit right in."

Fenstad wrote brochures in the publicity department of a computer company during the day, and taught an extension English-composition class at the downtown campus of the state university two nights a week. He didn't need the money; he taught the class because he liked teaching strangers and because he enjoyed the sense of hope that classrooms held for him. This hopefulness and didacticism he had picked up from his mother.

On Tuesday night she was standing at the door of the retirement apartment building, dressed in a dark blue overcoat—her best. Her stylishness was belied slightly by a pair of old fuzzy red earmuffs. Inside the car Fenstad noticed that she had put on perfume, unusual for her. Leaning back, she gazed out contentedly at the nighttime lights.

"Who's in this group of students?" she asked. "Working-class people, I hope. Those are the ones you should be teaching. Anything else is just a career."

"Oh, they work, all right." He looked at his mother and saw, as they passed under a streetlight, a combination of sadness and delicacy in her face. Her usual mask of tough optimism seemed to be deserting her. He braked at a red light and said, "I have a hairdresser and a garage mechanic and a housewife, a Mrs. Nelson, and three guys who're sanitation workers. Plenty of others. One guy you'll really like is a young black man with glasses who sits in the back row and reads *Workers' Vanguard* and Bakunin during class. He's brilliant. I don't know why he didn't test out of this class. His name's York Follette, and he's—"

"I want to meet him," she said quickly. She scowled at the moonlit snow. "A man with ideas. People like that have gone out of my life." She looked over at her son. "What I hate about being my age is how *nice* everyone tries to be. I was never nice, but now everybody is pelting me with sugar cubes." She opened her window an inch and let the cold air blow over her, ruffling her stiff gray hair.

When they arrived at the school, snow had started to fall, and at the other end of the parking lot a police car's flashing light beamed long crimson rays through the dense flakes. Fenstad's mother walked deliberately toward the door, shaking her head mistrustfully at the building and the police. Approaching the steps, she took her son's hand. "I liked the columns on the old buildings," she said, "the old university buildings, I mean. I liked Greek Revival better than this Modernist-bunker stuff." Inside, she blinked in the light at the smooth, waxed linoleum floors and cement-block walls. She held up her hand to shade her eyes. Fenstad took her elbow to guide her over the snow melting in puddles in the entryway. "I never asked you what you're teaching tonight."

"Logic," Fenstad said.

"Ah." She smiled and nodded. "Dialectics!"

"Not quite. Just logic."

She shrugged. She was looking at the clumps of students standing in the glare of the hallway, drinking coffee from paper cups and smoking cigarettes in the general conversational din. She wasn't used to such noise; she stopped in the middle of the corridor underneath a wall clock and stared happily in no particular direction. With her eyes shut she breathed in the close air smelling of wet overcoats and smoke, and Fenstad remembered how much his mother had always liked smoke-filled rooms, where ideas fought each other, and where some of those ideas died.

"Come on," he said, taking her hand again. Inside Fenstad's classroom six people sat in the angular postures of pre-boredom. York Follette was already in the back row, his copy of *Workers' Vanguard* shielding his face. Fenstad's mother headed straight for him and sat down in the desk next to his. Fenstad saw them shake hands, and in two minutes they were talking in low, rushed murmurs. He saw York Follette laugh quietly and nod. What was it that blacks saw and appreciated in his mother? They had always liked her—written to her, called her, checked up on her—and Fenstad wondered if they recognized something in his mother that he himself had never been able to see.

At 7:35 most of the students had arrived and were talking to each other vigorously, as if they didn't want Fenstad to start and thought they could delay him. He stared at them, and when they wouldn't quiet down, he made himself rigid and said, "Good evening. We have a guest tonight." Immediately the class grew silent. He held his arm out straight, indicating with a flick of his hand the old woman in the back row. "My mother," he said. "Clara Fenstad." For the first time all semester his students appeared to be paying attention; they turned around collectively and looked at Fenstad's mother, who smiled and waved. A few of the students began to applaud; others joined in. The applause was quiet but apparently genuine. Fenstad's mother brought herself slowly to her feet and made a suggestion of a bow. Two of the students sitting in front of her turned around and began to talk to her. At the front of the class Fenstad started his lecture on logic, but his mother wouldn't quiet down. This was a class for adults. They were free to do as they liked.

Lowering his head and facing the blackboard, Fenstad reviewed problems in logic, following point by point the outline set down by the textbook: *post hoc* fallacies, false authorities, begging the question, circular reasoning, *ad hominem* arguments, all the rest. Explaining these problems, his back turned, he heard sighs of boredom, boldly expressed. Occasionally he glanced at the back of the room. His mother was watching him carefully, and her face was expressing all the complexity of dismay. Dismay radiated from her. Her disappointment wasn't personal, because his mother didn't think that people as individuals were at fault for what they did. As usual, her disappointed hope was located in history and in the way people agreed with already existing histories.

She was angry with him for collaborating with grammar. She would call it unconsciously installed authority. Then she would find other names for it.

"All right," he said loudly, trying to make eye contact with someone in the room besides his mother, "let's try some examples. Can anyone tell me what, if anything, is wrong with the following sentence? 'I, like most people, have a unique problem.' "

The three sanitation workers, in the third row, began to laugh. Fenstad caught himself glowering and singled out the middle one.

"Yes, it is funny, isn't it?"

The man in the middle smirked and looked at the floor. "I was just thinking of my unique problem."

"Right," Fenstad said. "But what's wrong with saying, 'I, like most people, have a unique problem'?"

"Solving it?" This was Mrs. Nelson, who sat by the window so that she could gaze at the tree outside, lit by a streetlight. All through class she looked at the tree as if it were a lover.

"Solving what?"

"Solving the problem you have. What is the problem?"

"That's actually not what I'm getting at," Fenstad said. "Although it's a good *related* point. I'm asking what might be wrong logically with that sentence."

"It depends," Harold Ronson said. He worked in a service station and sometimes came to class wearing his work shirt with his name tag, HAROLD, stitched into it. "It depends on what your problem is. You haven't told us your problem."

"No," Fenstad said, "my problem is *not* the problem." He thought of Alice in Wonderland and felt, physically, as if he himself were getting small. "Let's try this again. What might be wrong with saying that most people have a unique problem?"

"You shouldn't be so critical," Timothy Melville said. "You should look on the bright side, if possible."

"What?"

"He's right," Mrs. Nelson said. "Most people have unique problems, but many people do their best to help themselves, such as taking night classes or working at meditation."

"No doubt that's true," Fenstad said. "But why can't most people have a unique problem?"

"Oh, I disagree," Mrs. Nelson said, still looking at her tree. Fenstad glanced at it and saw that it was crested with snow. It *was* beautiful. No wonder she looked at it. "I believe that most people do have unique problems. They just shouldn't talk about them all the time."

"Can anyone," Fenstad asked, looking at the back wall and hoping to see something there that was not wall, "can anyone give me an example of a unique problem?"

"Divorce," Barb Kjellerud said. She sat near the door and knitted during class. She answered questions without looking up. "Divorce is unique."

"No, it isn't!" Fenstad said, failing in the crucial moment to control his voice. He and his mother exchanged glances. In his mother's face for a split second was the history of her compassionate, ambivalent attention to him. "Divorce is not unique." He waited to calm himself. "It's everywhere. Now try again. Give me a unique problem."

Silence. "This is a trick question," Arlene Hubbly said. "I'm sure it's a trick question."

"Not necessarily. Does anyone know what *unique* means?"

"One of a kind," York Follette said, gazing at Fenstad with dry amusement. Sometimes he took pity on Fenstad and helped him out of jams. Fenstad's mother smiled and nodded.

"Right," Fenstad crowed, racing toward the blackboard as if he were about to write something. "So let's try again. Give me a unique problem."

"You give *us* a unique problem," one of the sanitation workers said. Fenstad didn't know whether he'd been given a statement or a command. He decided to treat it as a command.

"All right," he said. He stopped and looked down at his shoes. Maybe it *was* a trick question. He thought for ten seconds. Problem after problem presented itself to him. He thought of poverty, of the assaults on the earth, of the awful complexities of love. "I can't think of one," Fenstad said. His hands went into his pockets.

"That's because problems aren't personal," Fenstad's mother said from the back of the room. "They're collective." She waited while several students in the class sat up and nodded. "And people must work together on their solutions." She talked for another two minutes, taking the subject out of logic and putting it neatly in politics, where she knew it belonged.

The snow had stopped by the time the class was over. Fenstad took his mother's arm and escorted her to the car. After letting her down on the passenger side and starting the engine, he began to clear the front windshield. He didn't have a scraper and had forgotten his gloves, so he was using his bare hands. When he brushed the snow away on his mother's side, she looked out at him, surprised, a terribly aged Sleeping Beauty awakened against her will.

Once the car had warmed up, she was in a gruff mood and repositioned herself under the seat belt while making quiet but aggressive remarks. The sight of the new snow didn't seem to calm her. "Logic," she said at last. "That wasn't logic. Those are just rhetorical tactics. It's filler and drudgery."

"I don't want to discuss it now."

"All right. I'm sorry. Let's talk about something more pleasant."

They rode together in silence. Then she began to shake

her head. "Don't take me home," she said. "I want to have a spot of tea somewhere before I go back. A nice place where they serve tea, all right?"

He parked outside an all-night restaurant with huge front plate-glass windows; it was called Country Bob's. He held his mother's elbow from the car to the door. At the door, looking back to make sure that he had turned off his headlights, he saw his tracks and his mother's in the snow. His were separate footprints, but hers formed two long lines.

Inside, at the table, she sipped her tea and gazed at her son for a long time. "Thanks for the adventure, Harry. I do appreciate it. What're you doing in class next week? Oh, I remember. How-to papers. That should be interesting."

"Want to come?"

"Very much. I'll keep quiet next time, if you want me to."

Fenstad shook his head. "It's okay. It's fun having you along. You can say whatever you want. The students loved you. I knew you'd be a sensation, and you were. They'd probably rather have you teaching the class than me."

He noticed that his mother was watching something going on behind him, and Fenstad turned around in the booth so that he could see what it was. At first all he saw was a woman, a young woman with long hair wet from snow and hanging in clumps, talking in the aisle to two young men, both of whom were nodding at her. Then she moved on to the next table. She spoke softly. Fenstad couldn't hear her words, but he saw the solitary customer to whom she was speaking shake his head once, keeping his eyes down. Then the woman saw Fenstad and his mother. In a moment she was standing in front of them.

She wore two green plaid flannel shirts and a thin torn

jacket. Like Fenstad, she wore no gloves. Her jeans were patched, and she gave off a strong smell, something like hay, Fenstad thought, mixed with tar and sweat. He looked down at her feet and saw that she was wearing penny loafers with no socks. Coins, old pennies, were in both shoes; the leather was wet and cracked. He looked in the woman's face. Under a hat that seemed to collapse on either side of her head, the woman's face was thin and chalk-white except for the fatigue lines under her eyes. The eyes themselves were bright blue, beautiful, and crazy. To Fenstad, she looked desperate, percolating slightly with insanity, and he was about to say so to his mother when the woman bent down toward him and said, "Mister, can you spare any money?"

Involuntarily, Fenstad looked toward the kitchen, hoping that the manager would spot this person and take her away. When he looked back again, his mother was taking her blue coat off, wriggling in the booth to free her arms from the sleeves. Stopping and starting again, she appeared to be stuck inside the coat; then she lifted herself up, trying to stand, and with a quick, quiet groan slipped the coat off. She reached down and folded the coat over and held it toward the woman. "Here," she said. "Here's my coat. Take it before my son stops me."

"Mother, you can't." Fenstad reached forward to grab the coat, but his mother pulled it away from him.

When Fenstad looked back at the woman, her mouth was open, showing several gray teeth. Her hands were outstretched, and he understood, after a moment, that this was a posture of refusal, a gesture saying no, and that the woman wasn't used to it and did it awkwardly. Fenstad's mother was standing and trying to push the coat toward the woman, not toward her hands but lower, at waist level, and she was saying, "Here, here, here, here." The sound, like a human birdcall, frightened Fenstad, and he stood up quickly, reached for his wallet, and removed the first two bills he could find, two twenties. He grabbed the woman's chapped, ungloved left hand.

"Take these," he said, putting the two bills in her icy palm, "for the love of God, and please go."

He was close to her face. Tonight he would pray for her. For a moment the woman's expression was vacant. His mother was still pushing the coat at her, and the woman was unsteadily bracing herself. The woman's mouth was open, and her stagnant-water breath washed over him. "I know you," she said. "You're my little baby cousin."

"Go away, please," Fenstad said. He pushed at her. She turned, clutching his money. He reached around to put his hand on his mother's shoulders. "Ma," he said, "she's gone now. Mother, sit down. I gave her money for a coat." His mother fell down on her side of the booth, and her blue coat rolled over on the bench beside her, showing the label and the shiny inner lining. When he looked up, the woman who had been begging had disappeared, though he could still smell her odor, an essence of wretchedness.

"Excuse me, Harry," his mother said. "I have to go to the bathroom."

She rose and walked toward the front of the restaurant, turned a corner, and was out of sight. Fenstad sat and tried to collect himself. When the waiter came, a boy with an earring and red hair in a flattop, Fenstad just shook his head and said, "More tea." He realized that his mother hadn't taken off her earmuffs, and the image of his mother in the ladies' room with her earmuffs on gave him a fit of uneasiness. After getting up from the booth and following the path that his mother had taken, he stood outside the ladies'-room door and, when no one came in or out, he knocked. He waited for a decent interval. Still hearing no answer, he opened the door.

His mother was standing with her arms down on either side of the first sink. She was holding herself there, her eyes following the hot water as it poured from the tap around the bright porcelain sink down into the drain, and she looked furious. Fenstad touched her and she snapped toward him.

"Your logic!" she said.

He opened the door for her and helped her back to the booth. The second cup of tea had been served, and Fenstad's mother sipped it in silence. They did not converse. When she had finished, she said, "All right. I do feel better now. Let's go."

At the curb in front of her apartment building he leaned forward and kissed her on the cheek. "Pick me up next Tuesday," she said. "I want to go back to that class." He nodded. He watched as she made her way past the security guard at the front desk; then he put his car into drive and started home.

That night he skated in the dark for an hour with his friend, Susan, the pharmacist. She was an excellent skater; they had met on the ice. She kept late hours and, like Fenstad, enjoyed skating at night. She listened attentively to his story about his mother and the woman in the restaurant. To his great relief she recommended no course of action. She listened. She didn't believe in giving advice, even when asked.

The following Tuesday, Fenstad's mother was again in the back row next to York Follette. One of the fluorescent lights overhead was flickering, which gave the room, Fenstad thought, a sinister quality, like a debtors' prison or a refuge for the homeless. He'd been thinking about such people for the entire week. For seven days now he had caught whiffs of the woman's breath in the air, and one morning, Friday, he thought he caught a touch of the rotten-celery smell on his own breath, after a particularly difficult sales meeting.

Tonight was how-to night. The students were expected to stand at the front of the class and read their papers, instructing their peers and answering questions if necessary. Starting off, and reading her paper in a frightened monotone, Mrs. Nelson told the class how to bake a cheese soufflé. Arlene Hubbly's paper was about mushroom hunting. Fenstad was put off by the introduction. "The advantage to mushrooms," Arlene Hubbly read, "is that they are delicious. The disadvantage to mushrooms is that they can make you sick, even die." But then she explained how to recognize the common shaggymane by its cylindrical cap and dark tufts; she drew a model on the board. She warned the class against the *Clitocybe illudens,* the Jack-o'-Lantern. "Never eat a mushroom like this one or *any* mushroom that glows in the dark. Take heed!" she said, fixing her gaze on the class. Fenstad saw his mother taking rapid notes. Harold Ronson, the mechanic, reading his own prose painfully and slowly, told the class how to get rust spots out of their automobiles. Again Fenstad noticed his mother taking notes. York Follette told the class about the proper procedures for laying down attic insulation and how to know when enough was enough, so that a homeowner wouldn't be robbed blind, as he put it, by the salesmen, in whose ranks he had once counted himself.

Barb Kjellerud had brought along a cassette player and

told the class that her hobby was ballroom dancing; she would instruct them in the basic waltz. She pushed the play button on the tape machine, and "Tales from the Vienna Woods" came booming out. To the accompaniment of the music she read her paper, illustrating, as she went, how the steps were to be performed. She danced alone in front of them, doing so with flair. Her blonde hair swayed as she danced, Fenstad noticed. She looked a bit like a contestant in a beauty contest who had too much personality to win. She explained to the men the necessity of leading. Someone had to lead, she said, and tradition had given this responsibility to the male. Fenstad heard his mother snicker.

When Barb Kjellerud asked for volunteers, Fenstad's mother raised her hand. She said she knew how to waltz and would help out. At the front of the class she made a counterclockwise motion with her hand, and for the next minute, sitting at the back of the room, Fenstad watched his mother and one of the sanitation workers waltzing under the flickering fluorescent lights.

"What a wonderful class," Fenstad's mother said on the way home. "I hope you're paying attention to what they tell you."

Fenstad nodded. "Tea?" he asked.

She shook her head. "Where're you going after you drop me off?"

"Skating," he said. "I usually go skating. I have a date."

"With the pharmacist? In the dark?"

"We both like it, Ma." As he drove, he made an all-purpose gesture. "The moon and the stars," he said simply.

When he left her off, he felt unsettled. He considered, as a point of courtesy, staying with her a few minutes, but by the time he had this idea he was already away from the building and was headed down the street.

He and Susan were out on the ice together, skating in large circles, when Susan pointed to a solitary figure sitting on a park bench near the lake's edge. The sky had cleared; the moon gave everything a cold, fine-edged clarity. When Fenstad followed the line of Susan's finger, he saw at once that the figure on the bench was his mother. He realized it simply because of the way she sat there, drawn into herself, attentive even in the winter dark. He skated through the uncleared snow over the ice until he was standing close enough to speak to her. "Mother," he said, "what are you doing here?"

She was bundled up, a thick woolen cap drawn over her head, and two scarves covering much of her face. He could see little other than the two lenses of her glasses facing him in the dark. "I wanted to see you two," she told him. "I thought you'd look happy, and you did. I like to watch happiness. I always have."

"How can you see us? We're so far away."

"That's how I saw you."

This made no sense to him, so he asked, "How'd you get here?"

"I took a cab. That part was easy."

"Aren't you freezing?"

"I don't know. I don't know if I'm freezing or not."

He and Susan took her back to her apartment as soon as they could get their boots on. In the car Mrs. Fenstad insisted on asking Susan what kind of safety procedures were used to ensure that drugs weren't smuggled out of pharmacies and sold illegally, but she didn't appear to listen to the answer, and by the time they reached her building, she seemed to be falling asleep. They helped her up to her apartment. Susan thought that they should give her a warm bath before putting her to bed, and, together, they did. She did not protest. She didn't even seem to notice them as they guided her in and out of the bathtub.

Fenstad feared his mother would catch some lung infection, and it turned out to be bronchitis, which kept her in her apartment for the first three weeks of February, until her cough went down. Fenstad came by every other day to see how she was, and one Tuesday, after work, he went up to her floor and heard piano music: an old recording, which sounded much played, of the brightest and fastest jazz piano he had ever heard—music of superhuman brilliance. He swung open the door to her apartment and saw York Follette sitting near his mother's bed. On the bedside table was a small tape player, from which the music poured into the room.

Fenstad's mother was leaning back against the pillow, smiling, her eyes closed.

Follette turned toward Fenstad. He had been talking softly. He motioned toward the tape machine and said, "Art Tatum. It's a cut called 'Battery Bounce.' Your mother's never heard it."

"Jazz, Harry," Fenstad's mother said, her eyes still closed, not needing to see her son. "York is explaining to me about Art Tatum and jazz. Next week he's going to try something more progressive on me." Now his mother opened her eyes. "Have you ever heard such music before, Harry?"

They were both looking at him. "No," he said, "I never heard anything like it."

"This is my unique problem, Harry." Fenstad's mother coughed and then waited to recover her breath. "I never heard enough jazz." She smiled. "What glimpses!" she said at last.

After she recovered, he often found her listening to the tape machine that York Follette had given her. She liked to hear the Oscar Peterson Trio as the sun set and the lights of evening came on. She now often mentioned glimpses. Back at home, every night, Fenstad spoke about his mother in his prayers of remembrance and thanksgiving, even though he knew she would disapprove.

Happiness

Mary Lavin

Mother had a lot to say. This does not mean she was always talking but that we children felt the wells she drew upon were deep, deep, deep. Her theme was happiness: what it was, what it was not; where we might find it, where not; and how, if found, it must be guarded. Never must we confound it with pleasure. Nor think sorrow its exact opposite.

"Take Father Hugh." Mother's eyes flashed as she looked at him. "According to him, sorrow is an ingredient of happiness—a *necessary* ingredient, if you please." And when he tried to protest she put up her hand. "There may be a freakish truth in the theory—for some people. But not for me. And not, I hope, for my children." She looked severely at us three girls.

We laughed. None of us had had much experience with sorrow. Bea and I were children and Linda only a year old when our father died suddenly after a short illness that had not at first seemed serious. "I've known people to make sorrow a *substitute* for happiness," Mother said.

Father Hugh protested again. "You're not putting me in that class, I hope?"

Father Hugh, ever since our father died, had been the closest of anyone to us as a family, without being close to any one of us in particular—even to Mother. He lived in a monastery near our farm in County Meath, and he had been one of the celebrants at the Requiem High Mass our father's political importance had demanded. He met us that day for the first time, but he took to dropping in to see us, with the idea of filling the crater of loneliness left at our center. He did not know that there was a cavity in his own life, much less that we would fill it. He and Mother were both young in those days, and perhaps it gave scandal to some that he was so often in our house, staying till late into the night and, indeed, thinking nothing of stopping all night if there was any special reason, such as one of us being sick. He had even on occasion slept there if the night was too wet for tramping home across the fields.

When we girls were young, we were so used to having Father Hugh around that we never stood on ceremony with him but in his presence dried our hair and pared our nails and never minded what garments were strewn about. As for Mother—she thought nothing of running out of the bathroom in her slip, brushing her teeth or combing her hair, if she wanted to tell him something she might otherwise forget. And she brooked no criticism of her behavior. "Celibacy was never meant to take all the warmth and homeliness out of their lives," she said.

On this point, too, Bea was adamant. Bea, the middle sister, was our oracle. "I'm so glad he *has* Mother," she said, "as well as her having him, because it must be awful the way most women treat them—priests, I mean—as if they were pariahs. Mother treats him like a human being—that's all."

And when it came to Mother's ears that there had been gossip about her making free with Father Hugh, she opened her eyes wide in astonishment. "But he's only a priest!" she said.

Bea giggled. "It's a good job he didn't hear *that,*" she said to me afterwards. "It would undo the good she's done him. You'd think he was a eunuch."

"Bea!" I said. "Do you think he's in love with her?"

"If so, he doesn't know it," Bea said firmly. "It's her soul he's after! Maybe he wants to make sure of her in the next world!"

But thoughts of the world to come never troubled Mother. "If anything ever happens to me, children," she said, "suddenly, I mean, or when you are not near me, or I cannot speak to you, I want you to promise you won't feel bad. There's no need! Just remember that I had a happy life—and that if I had to choose my kind of heaven I'd take it on this earth with you again, no matter how much you might annoy me!"

You see, annoyance and fatigue, according to Mother, and even illness and pain, could coexist with happiness. She had a habit of asking people if they were happy at times and in places that—to say the least of it—seemed to us inappropriate. "But are you happy?" she'd probe as one lay sick and bathed in sweat, or in the throes of a jumping toothache. And once in our presence she made the inquiry of an old friend as he lay upon his deathbed.

"Why not?" she said when we took her to task for it later. "Isn't it more important than ever to be happy when you're dying? Take my own father! You know what he said in his last moments? On his deathbed, he defied me to name a man who had enjoyed a better life. In spite of dreadful pain, his face *radiated* happiness!" Mother nodded her head comfortably. "Happiness drives out pain, as fire burns out fire."

Having no knowledge of our own to pit against hers, we thirstily drank in her rhetoric. Only Bea was sceptical. "Perhaps you *got* it from him, like spots, or fever," she said. "Or something that could at least be slipped from hand to hand."

"Do you think I'd have taken it if that were the case!" Mother cried. "Then, when he needed it most?"

"Not there and then!" Bea said stubbornly. "I meant as a sort of legacy."

"Don't you think in *that* case," Mother said, exasperated, "he would have felt obliged to leave it to your grandmother?"

Certainly we knew that in spite of his lavish heart our grandfather had failed to provide our grandmother with enduring happiness. He had passed that job on to Mother. And Mother had not made too good a fist of it, even when Father was living and she had him—and later, us children—to help.

As for Father Hugh, he had given our grandmother up early in the game. "God Almighty couldn't make that woman happy," he said one day, seeing Mother's face, drawn and pale with fatigue, preparing for the nightly run over to her own mother's flat that would exhaust her utterly.

There were evenings after she came home from the library where she worked when we saw her stand with the car keys in her hand, trying to think which would be worse—to slog over there on foot, or take out the car again. And yet the distance was short. It was Mother's day that had been too long.

"Weren't you over to see her this morning?" Father Hugh demanded.

"No matter!" said Mother. She was no doubt thinking of the forlorn face our grandmother always put on when she was leaving. ("Don't say good night, Vera," Grandmother would plead. "It makes me feel too lonely. And you never can tell—you might slip over again before you go to bed!")

"Do you know the time?" Bea would say impatiently, if she happened to be with Mother. Not indeed that the lateness of the hour counted for anything, because in all likelihood Mother *would* go back, if only to pass by under the window and see that the lights were out, or stand and listen and make sure that as far as she could tell all was well.

"I wouldn't mind if she was happy," Mother said.

"And how do you know she's not?" we'd ask.

"When people are happy, I can feel it. Can't you?"

We were not sure. Most people thought our grandmother was a gay creature, a small birdy being who even at a great age laughed like a girl, and—more remarkably—sang like one, as she went about her day. But beak and claw were of steel. She'd think nothing of sending Mother back to a shop three times if her errands were not exactly right. "Not sugar like that—that's *too* fine; it's not castor sugar I want. But *not* as coarse as *that,* either. I want an in-between kind."

Provoked one day, my youngest sister, Linda, turned and gave battle. "You're mean!" she cried. "You love ordering people about!"

Grandmother preened, as if Linda had acclaimed an attribute. "I was always hard to please," she said. "As a girl, I used to be called Miss Imperious."

And Miss Imperious she remained as long as she lived, even when she was a great age. Her orders were then given a wry twist by the fact that as she advanced in age she took to calling her daughter Mother, as we did.

There was one great phrase with which our grandmother opened every sentence: "if only." "If only," she'd say, when we came to visit her—"if only you'd come earlier, before I was worn out expecting you!" Or if we were early, then if only it was later, after she'd had a rest and could enjoy us, be *able* for us. And if we brought her flowers, she'd sigh to think that if only we'd brought them the previous day she'd have had a visitor to appreciate them, or say it was a pity the stems weren't longer. If only we'd picked a few green leaves, or included some buds, because, she said disparagingly, the poor flowers we'd brought were already wilting. We might just as well not have brought them! As the years went on, Grandmother had a new bead to add to her rosary: if only her friends were not all dead! By their absence, they reduced to nil all *real* enjoyment in anything. Our own father—her son-in-law—was the one person who had ever gone close to pleasing her. But even here there had been a snag. "If only he was my real son!" she used to say with a sigh.

Mother's mother lived on through our childhood and into our early maturity (though she outlived the money our grandfather left her), and in our minds she was a complicated mixture of valiance and defeat. Courageous and generous within the limits of her own life, her simplest demand was yet enormous in the larger frame of Mother's life, and so we never could see her with the same clarity of vision with which we saw our grandfather, or our own father. Them we saw only through Mother's eyes.

"Take your grandfather!" she'd cry, and instantly we'd

see him, his eyes burning upon us—yes, upon *us,* although in his day only one of us had been born: me. At another time, Mother would cry, "Take your own father!" and instantly we'd see *him*—tall, handsome, young, and much more suited to marry one of us than poor bedraggled Mother.

Most fascinating of all were the times Mother would say "Take me!" By magic then, staring down the years, we'd see blazingly clear a small girl with black hair and buttoned boots, who, though plain and pouting, burned bright, like a star. "I was happy, you see," Mother said. And we'd strain hard to try and understand the mystery of the light that still radiated from her. "I used to lean along a tree that grew out over the river," she said, "and look down through the gray leaves at the water flowing past below, and I used to think it was not the stream that flowed but me, spread-eagled over it, who flew through the air! Like a bird! That I'd found the secret!" She made it seem there might *be* such a secret, just waiting to be found. Another time she'd dream that she'd be a great singer.

"We didn't know you sang, Mother!"

She had to laugh. "Like a crow," she said.

Sometimes she used to think she'd swim the Channel.

"Did you swim *that* well, Mother?"

"Oh, not really—just the breast stroke," she said. "And then only by the aid of two pig bladders blown up by my father and tied around my middle. But I used to throb—yes, throb—with happiness."

Behind Mother's back, Bea raised her eyebrows.

What was it, we used to ask ourselves—that quality that she, we felt sure, misnamed? Was it courage? Was it strength, health, or high spirits? Something you could not give or take—a conundrum? A game of catch-as-you-can?

"I know," cried Bea. "A sham!"

Whatever it was, we knew that Mother would let no wind of violence from within or without tear it from her. Although, one evening when Father Hugh was with us, our astonished ears heard her proclaim that there might be a time when one had to slacken hold on it—let go—to catch at it again with a surer hand. In the way, we supposed, that the high-wire walker up among the painted stars of his canvas sky must wait to fling himself through the air until the bar he catches at has started to sway perversely from him. Oh no, no! That downward drag at our innards we could not bear, the belly swelling to the shape of a pear. Let happiness go by the board. "After all, lots of people seem to make out without it," Bea cried. It was too tricky a business. And might it not be that one had to be born with a flair for it?

"A flair would not be enough," Mother answered. "Take Father Hugh. He, if anyone, had a flair for it—a natural capacity! You've only to look at him when he's off guard, with you children, or helping me in the garden. But he rejects happiness! He casts it from him."

"That is simply not true, Vera," cried Father Hugh, overhearing her. "It's just that I don't place an inordinate value on it like you. I don't think it's enough to carry one all the way. To the end, I mean—and after."

"Oh, don't talk about the end when we're only in the middle," cried Mother. And, indeed, at that moment her own face shone with such happiness it was hard to believe that earth was not her heaven. Certainly it was her constant contention that of happiness she had had a lion's share. This, however, we, in private, doubted. Perhaps there were times when she had had a surplus of it—when she was young, say, with her redoubtable father, whose love blazed circles around her, making winter into summer and ice into fire. Perhaps she did have a brimming measure in her early married years. By straining hard, we could find traces left in our minds from those days of milk and honey. Our father, while he lived, had cast a magic over everything, for us as well as for her. He held his love up over us like an umbrella and kept off the troubles that afterwards came down on us, pouring cats and dogs!

But if she did have more than the common lot of happiness in those early days, what use was that when we could remember so clearly how our father's death had ravaged her? And how could we forget the distress it brought on us when, afraid to let her out of our sight, Bea and I stumbled after her everywhere, through the woods and along the bank of the river, where, in the weeks that followed, she tried vainly to find peace.

The summer after Father died, we were invited to France to stay with friends, and when she went walking on the cliffs at Fécamp our fears for her grew frenzied, so that we hung on to her arm and dragged at her skirt, hoping that like leaded weights we'd pin her down if she went too near to the edge. But at night we had to abandon our watch, being forced to follow the conventions of a family still whole—a home still intact—and go to bed at the same time as the other children. It was at that hour, when the coast guard was gone from his rowing boat offshore and the sand was as cold and gray as the sea, that Mother liked to swim. And when she had washed, kissed, and left us, our hearts almost died inside us and we'd creep out of bed again to stand in our bare feet at the mansard and watch as she ran down the shingle, striking out when she reached the water where, far out, wave and sky and mist were one, and the grayness closed over her. If we took our eyes off her for an instant, it was impossible to find her again.

"Oh, make her turn back, God, please!" I prayed out loud one night.

Startled, Bea turned away from the window. "She'll *have* to turn back sometime, won't she? Unless . . . ?"

Locking our damp hands together, we stared out again. "She wouldn't!" I whispered. "It would be a sin!"

Secure in the deterring power of sin, we let out our breath. Then Bea's breath caught again. "What if she went out so far she used up all her strength? She couldn't swim back! It wouldn't be a sin then!"

"It's the intention that counts," I whispered.

A second later, we could see an arm lift heavily up and wearily cleave down, and at last Mother was in the shallows, wading back to shore.

"Don't let her see us!" cried Bea. As if our chattering teeth would not give us away when she looked in at us before she went to her own room on the other side of the corridor, where, later in the night, sometimes the sound of crying would reach us.

What was it worth—a happiness bought that dearly.

Mother had never questioned it. And once she told us, "On a wintry day, I brought my own mother a snowdrop. It was the first one of the year—a bleak bud that had come up stunted before its time—and I meant it for a sign. But do you know what your grandmother said? "What good are snowdrops to me now?" Such a thing to say! What good is a snowdrop at all if it doesn't hold its value always, and never lose it! Isn't that the whole point of a snowdrop? And that is the whole point of happiness, too! What good would it be if it could be erased without trace? Take me and those daffodils!" Stooping, she buried her face in a bunch that lay on the table waiting to be put in vases. "If they didn't hold their beauty absolute and inviolable, do you think I could bear the sight of them after what happened when your father was in hospital?"

It was a fair question. When Father went to hospital, Mother went with him and stayed in a small hotel across the street so she could be with him all day from early to late. "Because it was so awful for him—being in Dublin!" she said. "You have no idea how he hated it."

That he was dying neither of them realized. How could they know, as it rushed through the sky, that their star was a falling star! But one evening when she'd left him asleep Mother came home for a few hours to see how we were faring, and it broke her heart to see the daffodils out all over the place—in the woods, under the trees, and along the sides of the avenue. There had never been so many, and she thought how awful it was that Father was missing them. "You sent up little bunches to him, you poor dears!" she said. "Sweet little bunches, too—squeezed tight as posies by your little fists! But stuffed into vases they couldn't really make up to him for not being able to see them growing!"

So on the way back to the hospital she stopped her car and pulled a great bunch—the full of her arms. "They took up the whole back seat," she said, "and I was so excited at the thought of walking into his room and dumping them on his bed—you know—just plomping them down so he could smell them, and feel them, and look and look! I didn't mean them to be put in vases, or anything ridiculous like that—it would have taken a rainwater barrel to hold them. Why, I could hardly see over them as I came up the steps; I kept tripping. But when I came into the hall, that nun—I told you about her—that nun came up to me, sprang out of nowhere it seemed, although I know now that she was waiting for me, knowing that somebody had to bring me to my senses. But the way she did it! Reached out and grabbed the flowers, letting lots of them fall—I remember them getting stood on. 'Where are you going with those foolish flowers, you foolish woman?' she said. 'Don't you know your husband is dying? Your prayers are all you can give him now!' "

"She was right. I *was* foolish. But I wasn't cured. Afterwards, it was nothing but foolishness the way I dragged you children after me all over Europe. As if any one place was going to be different from another, any better, any less desolate. But there was great satisfaction in bringing you places your father and I had planned to bring you—although in fairness to him I must say that he would not perhaps have brought you so young. And he would not have had an ulterior motive. But above all, he would not have attempted those trips in such a dilapidated car."

Oh, that car! It was a battered and dilapidated red sports car, so depleted of accessories that when, eventually, we got a new car Mother still stuck out her hand on bends, and in wet weather jumped out to wipe the windscreen with her sleeve. And if fussed, she'd let down the window and shout at people, forgetting she now had a horn. How we had ever fitted into it with all our luggage was a miracle.

"You were never lumpish—any of you!" Mother said proudly. "But you were very healthy and very strong." She turned to me. "Think of how you got that car up the hill in Switzerland!"

"The Alps are not hills, Mother!" I pointed out coldly, as I had done at the time, when, as actually happened, the car failed to make it on one of the inclines. Mother let it run back until it wedged against the rock face, and I had to get out and push till she got going again in first gear. But when it got started it couldn't be stopped to pick me up until it got to the top, where they had to wait for me, and for a very long time.

"Ah, well," she said, sighing wistfully at the thought of those trips. "You got something out of them, I hope. All that traveling must have helped you with your geography and your history."

We looked at each other and smiled, and then Mother herself laughed. "Remember the time," she said, "when we were in Italy, and it was Easter, and all the shops were chock-full of food? The butchers' shops had poultry and game hanging up outside the doors, fully feathered, and with their poor heads dripping blood, and in the windows they had poor little lambs and suckling pigs and young goats, all skinned and hanging by their hindfeet." Mother shuddered. "They think so much about food. I found it revolting. I had to hurry past. But Linda, who must have been only four then, dragged at me and stared and stared. You know how children are at that age; they have a morbid fascination for what is cruel and bloody. Her face was flushed and her eyes were wide. I hurried her back to the hotel. But next morning she crept into my room. She crept up to me and pressed against me. 'Can't we go back, just once, and look again at that shop?' she whispered. 'The shop where they have the little children hanging up for Easter!' It was the young goats, of course, but I'd said 'kids,' I suppose. How we laughed." But her face was grave. "You were *so* good on those trips, all of you," she said. "You were really very good children in general. Otherwise I would never have put so much effort into rearing you, because I wasn't a bit maternal. You brought out the best in me! I put an unnatural effort into you, of course, because I was taking my standards from your father, forgetting that his might not have remained so inflexible if he had lived to middle age and was beset by life, like other parents."

"Well, the job is nearly over now, Vera," said Father Hugh. "And you didn't do so badly."

"That's right, Hugh," said Mother, and she straightened up, and put her hand to her back the way she sometimes did in the garden when she got up from her knees after weeding. "I didn't go over to the enemy anyway! We survived!" Then a flash of defiance came into her eyes. "And we were happy. That's the main thing!"

Father Hugh frowned. "There you go again!" he said.

Mother turned on him. "I don't think you realize the onslaughts that were made upon our happiness! The minute Robert died, they came down on me—cohorts of relatives, friends, even strangers, all draped in black, opening their arms like bats to let me pass into their company. 'Life is a vale of tears,' they said. 'You are privileged to find it out so young!' Ugh! After I staggered on to my feet and began to take hold of life once more, they fell back defeated. And the first day I gave a laugh—pouff, they were blown out like candles. They weren't living in a real world at all; they belonged to a ghostly world where life was easy: all one had to do was sit and weep. It takes effort to push back the stone from the mouth of the tomb and walk out."

Effort. Effort. Ah, but that strange-sounding word could invoke little sympathy from those who had not learned yet what it meant. Life must have been hardest for Mother in those years when we older ones were at college—no longer children, and still dependent on her. Indeed, we made more demands on her than ever then, having moved into new areas of activity and emotion. And our friends! Our friends came and went as freely as we did ourselves, so that the house was often like a café—and one where pets were not prohibited but took their places on our chairs and beds, as regardless as the people. And anyway it was hard to have sympathy for someone who got things into such a state as Mother. All over the house there was clutter. Her study was like the returned-letter department of a post-office, with stacks of paper everywhere, bills paid and unpaid, letters answered and unanswered, tax returns, pamphlets, leaflets. If by mistake we left the door open on a windy day, we came back to find papers flapping through the air like frightened birds. Efficient only in that she managed eventually to conclude every task she began, it never seemed possible to outsiders that by Mother's methods anything whatever could be accomplished. In an attempt to keep order elsewhere, she made her own room the clearing house into which the rest of us put everything: things to be given away, things to be mended, things to be stored, things to be treasured, things to be returned—even things to be thrown out! By the end of the year, the room resembled an obsolescence dump. And no one could help her; the chaos of her life was as personal as an act of creation—one might as well try to finish another person's poem.

As the years passed, Mother rushed around more hectically. And although Bea and I had married and were not at home any more, except at holiday time and for occasional weekends, Linda was noisier than the two of us put together had been, and for every follower we had brought home she brought twenty. The house was never still. Now that we were reduced to being visitors, we watched Mother's tension mount to vertigo, knowing that, like a spinning top, she could not rest till she fell. But now at the smallest pretext Father Hugh would call in the doctor and Mother would be put on the mail boat and dispatched for London. For it was essential that she get far enough away to make phoning home every night prohibitively costly.

Unfortunately, the thought of departure often drove a spur into her and she redoubled her effort to achieve order in her affairs. She would be up until the early hours ransacking her desk. To her, as always, the shortest parting entailed a preparation as for death. And as if it were her end that was at hand, we would all be summoned, although she had no time to speak a word to us, because five minutes before departure she would still be attempting to reply to letters that were the acquisition of weeks and would have taken whole days to dispatch.

"Don't you know the taxi is at the door, Vera?" Father Hugh would say, running his hand through his gray hair and looking very disheveled himself. She had him at times as distracted as herself. "You can't do any more. You'll have to leave the rest till you come back."

"I can't, I can't!" Mother would cry. "I'll have to cancel my plans."

One day, Father Hugh opened the lid of her case, which was strapped up in the hall, and with a swipe of his arm he cleared all the papers on the top of the desk pell-mell into the suitcase. "You can sort them on the boat," he said, "or the train to London!"

Thereafter, Mother's luggage always included an empty case to hold the unfinished papers on her desk. And years afterwards a steward on the Irish Mail told us she was a familiar figure, working away at letters and bills nearly all the way from Holyhead to Euston. "She gave it up about Rugby or Crewe," he said. "She'd get talking to someone in the compartment." He smiled. "There was one time coming down the train I was just in time to see her close up the window with a guilty look. I didn't say anything, but I think she'd emptied those papers of hers out the window!"

Quite likely. When we were children, even a few hours away from us gave her composure. And in two weeks or less, when she'd come home, the well of her spirit would be freshened. We'd hardly know her—her step so light, her eye so bright, and her love and patience once more freely flowing. But in no time at all the house would fill up once more with the noise and confusion of too many people and too many animals, and again we'd be fighting our corner with cats and dogs, bats, mice, bees and even wasps. "Don't kill it!" Mother would cry if we raised a hand to an angry wasp. "Just catch it, dear, and put it outside. Open the window and let it fly away!" But even this treatment could at times be deemed too harsh. "Wait a minute. Close the window!" she'd cry. "It's too cold outside. It will die. That's why it came in, I suppose! Oh dear, what will we do?" Life would be going full blast again.

There was only one place Mother found rest. When she was at breaking point and fit to fall, she'd go out into the garden—not to sit or stroll around but to dig, to drag up weeds, to move great clumps of corms or rhizomes, or indeed quite frequently to haul huge rocks from one place to another. She was always laying down a path, building a dry wall, or making compost heaps as high as hills. However jaded she might be going out, when dark forced her in at last her step had the spring of a daisy. So if she did not succeed in defining happiness to our understanding, we could see that whatever it was, she possessed it to the full when she was in her garden.

One of us said as much one Sunday when Bea and I had dropped round for the afternoon. Father Hugh was with us again. "It's an unthinking happiness, though," he cavilled. We were standing at the drawing-room window, looking out to where in the fading light we could see Mother on her knees weeding, in the long border that stretched from the house right down to the woods. "I wonder how she'd take it if she were stricken down and had to give up that heavy work!" he said. Was he perhaps a little jealous of how she could stoop and bend? He himself had begun to use a stick. I was often a little jealous of her myself, because although I was married and had children of my own, I had married young and felt the weight of living as heavy as a weight of years. "She doesn't take enough care of herself," Father Hugh said sadly. "Look at her out there with nothing under her knees to protect her from the damp ground." It was almost too dim for us to see her, but even in the drawing-room it was chilly. "She should not be let stay out there after the sun goes down."

"Just you try to get her in then!" said Linda, who had come into the room in time to hear him. "Don't you know by now anyway that what would kill another person only seems to make Mother thrive?"

Father Hugh shook his head again. "You seem to forget it's not younger she's getting!" He fidgeted and fussed, and several times went to the window to stare out apprehensively. He was really getting quite elderly.

"Come and sit down, Father Hugh," Bea said, and to take his mind off Mother she turned on the light and blotted out the garden. Instead of seeing through the window, we saw into it as into a mirror, and there between the flower-laden tables and lamps it was ourselves we saw moving vaguely. Like Father Hugh, we, too, were waiting for her to come in before we called an end to the day.

"Oh, this is ridiculous!" Father Hugh cried at last. "She'll have to listen to reason." And going back to the window he threw it open. "Vera!" he called. "Vera!"—sternly, so sternly that, more intimate than an endearment, his tone shocked us. "She didn't hear me," he said, turning back blinking at us in the lighted room. "I'm going out to get her." And in a minute he was gone from the room. As he ran down the garden path, we stared at each other, astonished; his step, like his voice, was the step of a lover. "I'm coming, Vera!" he cried.

Although she was never stubborn except in things that mattered, Mother had not moved. In the wholehearted way she did everything, she was bent down close to the ground. It wasn't the light only that was dimming; her eyesight also was failing, I thought, as instinctively I followed Father Hugh.

But halfway down the path I stopped. I had seen something he had not: Mother's hand that appeared to support itself in a forked branch of an old tree peony she had planted as a bride was not in fact gripping it but impaled upon it. And the hand that appeared to be grubbing in the clay in fact was sunk into the soft molding. "Mother!" I screamed, and I ran forward, but when I reached her I covered my face with my hands. "Oh Father Hugh!" I cried. "Is she dead?"

It was Bea who answered, hysterical. "She is! She is!" she cried, and she began to pound Father Hugh on the back with her fists, as if his pessimistic words had made this happen.

But Mother was not dead. And at first the doctor even

offered hope of her pulling through. But from the moment Father Hugh lifted her up to carry her into the house we ourselves had no hope, seeing how effortlessly he, who was not strong, could carry her. When he put her down on her bed, her head hardly creased the pillow. Mother lived for four more hours.

Like the days of her life, those four hours that Mother lived were packed tight with concern and anxiety. Partly conscious, partly delirious, she seemed to think the counterpane was her desk, and she scrabbled her fingers upon it as if trying to sort out a muddle of bills and correspondence. No longer indifferent now, we listened, anguished, to the distracted cries that had for all our lifetime been so familiar to us. "Oh, where is it? Where is it? I had it a minute ago! Where on earth did I put it?"

"Vera, Vera, stop worrying," Father Hugh pleaded, but she waved him away and went on sifting through the sheets as if they were sheets of paper. "Oh, Vera!" he begged. "Listen to me. Do you not know—"

Bea pushed between them. "You're not to tell her!" she commanded. "Why frighten her?"

"But it ought not to frighten her," said Father Hugh. "This is what I was always afraid would happen—that she'd be frightened when it came to the end."

At that moment, as if to vindicate him, Mother's hands fell idle on the coverlet, palm upward and empty. And turning her head she stared at each of us in turn, beseechingly. "I cannot face it," she whispered. "I can't! I can't! I can't!"

"Oh, my God!" Bea said, and she started to cry.

"Vera. For God's sake listen to me," Father Hugh cried, and pressing his face to hers, as close as a kiss, he kept whispering to her, trying to cast into the dark tunnel before her the light of his own faith.

But it seemed to us that Mother must already be looking into God's exigent eyes. "I can't!" she cried. "I can't!"

Then her mind came back from the stark world of the spirit to the world where her body was still detained, but even that world was now a whirling kaleidoscope of things which only she could see. Suddenly her eyes focused, and, catching at Father Hugh, she pulled herself up a little and pointed to something we could not see. "What will be done with them?" Her voice was anxious. "They ought to be put in water anyway," she said, and leaning over the edge of the bed, she pointed to the floor. "Don't step on that one!" she said sharply. Then more sharply still, she addressed us all. "Have them sent to the public ward," she said peremptorily. "Don't let that nun take them; she'll only put them on the altar. And God doesn't want them! He made them for *us*—not for Himself!"

It was the familiar rhetoric that all her life had characterized her utterances. For a moment we were mystified. Then Bea gasped. "The daffodils!" she cried. "The day Father died!" And over her face came the light that had so often blazed over Mother's. Leaning across the bed, she pushed Father Hugh aside. And, putting out her hands, she held Mother's face between her palms as tenderly as if it were the face of a child. "It's all right, Mother. You don't *have* to face it! It's over!" Then she who had so fiercely forbade Father Hugh to do so blurted out the truth. "You've finished with this world, Mother," she said, and, confident that her tidings were joyous, her voice was strong.

Mother made the last effort of her life and grasped at

Bea's meaning. She let out a sigh, and, closing her eyes, she sank back, and this time her head sank so deep into the pillow that it would have been dented had it been a pillow of stone.

Songs My Mother Taught Me

Hortense Calisher

Some ten years ago when I was for the first time in London—when, as a rather elderly innocent abroad, I was for the first time *any*where outside New York City except Rochester, Elmira, Binghamton, the Eastern Shore, a few summer resorts in New England and, at the age of twelve, Asbury Park, New Jersey—I attended a semi-diplomatic dinner party at which, after we had all drunk considerable amounts of several delightful wines, one of the ladies present suddenly peeled off her blouse.

Since the other guests, though moist and perfervid, were still upright in their chairs and conversation, the incident caused, even in that imperturbable company, a certain silence.

Chitchat, suddenly quenched, faded off into one of those pauses where isolated sentences stand out sharply. The man on my left, whom I had placed tentatively as either a connoisseur of heraldry or a baiter of Americans, had been lecturing me on the purity of lineage maintained by German nobility up to the last war. "Where else," he had just inquired, "can one find, even now, a person whose line shows sixteen quarterings?" Then he stopped short, as if contradicted by circumstance. Headily I reassured myself that quite without knowing it—and in the first week too—I must have scaled one of those dizzily international heights of society so often promised the provincial: a set so patrician that queens had no legs, emperors might be clothed exactly as they said they were, and ladies appeared in their quarterings without shame.

She was an exceedingly pretty young woman of about twenty-five with masses of blond hair arranged ingénue, and a pair of truly enormous blue eyes swimming in some Venus-lymph, clear natural nacre in which a man, or indeed any onlooker, might well sink. Words like "truly" came inevitably to mind as one regarded them. As I did so, they spilled over pellucidly. Casting a reproachful look at her partner (later it was understood that he had dared her), turning down the corners of a lovely mouth rosied with wine and—though one hated to think it—stupidity, she gazed at us, clutching the discarded portion of her costume, then hung her head and let fall on her lavishly ruffled *broderie anglaise* corselet two neatly schooled tears.

"Why, Lady Catherine!" our host said at once, and rising, he went round the table to her and poured her more wine, murmuring what I thought to be "How very sporting!" and capping it with—as he raised his own glass—"Bravo!"

Other gentlemen took up the plaudit. Lady Catherine, shyly consoled, raised her head, and I remembered her patronymic, ducally familiar even to me: one of her ancestresses, whom she was said to resemble, had been a wife of Henry the Eighth. From her round eyes two more pearls dropped, but this time surely with retrospective art—I wondered whether Henry, watching her ancestress' head fall, might not have thought to himself, "None of my other wives looked that good upside down."

What happened next I can only recount, not explain. It is true that, while we were only fourteen at table, the number of empty bottles ranged testimonially behind us must have totaled more than twice that. I have a vague impression that the male applause may have attained an ethnic intensity. Also that our host, bending over Lady Catherine, was assuring her that she looked smashing, and rather more respectable than the portrait of his grandmother as lady in waiting to Queen Alexandra. And that she, though retaining a disconsolate posture, was looking smug. What I know for sure is that when I next glanced at our hostess—a bishop's daughter—she too had peeled.

"She's upset the gravy boat, Mother!" I murmured delightedly, but of course no one paid any attention to me, or would have understood the reference if they had. No one there was likely to have heard of Mrs. Potter Palmer, much less of my mother. I shall shortly explain—for the benefit of readers who, although they may have caught the allusion to American social history, cannot possibly know anything of mine. But first let me complete the mise-en-scène of a moment in which were to be brought home to me all the old saws of my girlhood—a moment of truth in which, across so much water and over the ten years of my mother's sojourn in Mrs. Grundy's heaven, I could at last exclaim to her, "Mother, you were right!"

Of the seven women at table, six, including myself, were wearing the version of the currently fashionable (and easily doffable) "separates" known as "evening sweaters." There was nothing coincidental about this; the best houses were cold, even for London; rationing was still on and the English were burning an ineffectual sludge called, with their usual talent, "nutty slack." The one exception to the sweaters was also the only one of the others who was neither chic nor pretty, a vast, untidy woman opposite me—Frau Ewig, a noted anthropologist, recently returned from Sierra Leone—whose dress, showing so many possible means of separation that the eye was unable to choose the probable, looked somewhat as if, in order to appear in it at the party, she had first chopped several natives up. She, like the rest of us, had forgotten Lady Catherine in the sight of our hostess, who sat revealed, with the air of a prioress who had removed her wimple, in a rock-pink, ten-guinea model by Berlé.

In the silence that followed I heard the clink of crystal—the gentlemen, according to their needs and natures, were either taking another drink or putting down the one they had. A muted cry of protest was heard—from Lady Catherine. I could have seconded it—for another reason. For glancing round at the other ladies, I sensed something infinitely feminine glissade from eye to eye. In prescience I closed mine. When I opened them, what I saw confirmed it. Every remaining lady—except the anthropologist and the American—had the upper part of her costume in her hand.

Now there was nothing essentially risky in the tableau before us: a number of ladies sitting, modestly swan-necked, in their foundations, is a sight familiar to every window-shopper. Besides, the temperature being what it was, I thought I could discern, between various lacy interstices, the fuzzier-than-flesh-tone of what Debenham & Freebody's (where I bought one the next morning) called a vest. No, the riskiness is often in the eye of the beholder. And this composite eye, twelve times magnified and stern as that of a nudist group eying the indecency of a visitor's clothing, was now fixed on my pied vis-à-vis and on me. Leave me there now, while we make our way back—by gravy boat and a sneaky trail of safety pins—to my mother. We shall return.

Moral instruction by moral illustration has long since disappeared from the training of the young. Metaphor itself is considered untrustworthy—likely to weaken the facts of what already is a pretty slippery reality—and every good parent knows that the parable is too "punitive" by far. My childhood was full of them, from boogieman to Bunyan, my parents belonging to a generation still very sure of its facts. And my mother's specialty was what might be called the "social" allegory. Obvious in design, single in target, it was part of the process by which she hoped to transform the unpromising grub at that very moment scratching its knee-scabs in front of her into something pretty and marriageable, designed to preside, with some of her own graces and others she aspired to, at a table even more elaborate than her own.

Under a codex possibly marked "Accidents, Dinner"—for, as will be seen, a good proportion of my mother's tales revolved on accident—reposed Mrs. Potter Palmer. Famous arbiter of bygone Chicago society, she may be the model for performances slightly more rarefied than the one I know her for—as for me, I see her only in the attitude of one. Eternally she presides at her exalted dinner table, from whose foot, in the worm's-eye view of my mother's imagination, she is all but obscured by the gravy boat suited to her station—to my mind about twice the size of our largest tureen. In her historic moment she knows nothing of us, but all is open to posterity—hovering above her now like helicopters, like damsel flies, we see all. Then it happens. Far down the length of the gilt-encrusted table—exactly center I make it for drama—a guest jars a servingman's wrist. A great gout of gravy erupts on the cloth.

My mother pauses; I return her look of high seriousness. Extrasensory perception or what you will, with not a word said between us, our images of that cloth are the same. As a superb embroiderer, my mother's chef d'oeuvre is her banquet cloth. Loaded with eyelet, scallop, punchwork, Valenciennes, fringe and insertion, lying even now on its cardboard cylinder between sheets of preservative blue paper, five years in the making, never used and none like it in the world—yet there on that august table, with a terrible brown blot on its middle, lies its twin.

The guest hangs his head, and no wonder. In unavoidable frisson the other guests, well-bred as they are, avert theirs. We gloat over the dreadful moment, knowing rescue is nigh. Mrs. Palmer, whose eagle eye—exactly like my mother's at her half-yearly dinner parties—sees everything while appearing to register nothing, pauses for a fraction in her elegant conversation. Then she makes her gesture—irreparable and immortal. I see her elbow, plump, white and shapely, a noble fin-de-siècle elbow suited to its duty, not covered with chicken-skin like mine. Carefully careless as Réjane, no doubt chatting gaily the while, she has swept it outward. Hail Mrs. Palmer, heroic hostess, who, in the imitation that is the ultimate of good manners, is seen now to have overturned, on that cloth, the tureen!

With years of reflection, this tale of my mother's, like another even more pertinent, came to have as many holes in it as the cloth had eyelets. Was it quite the thing to be so exemplary so publicly? Wouldn't the real acme of taste have been not to notice—had the guest felt better, or worse? It came to me that Mrs. Palmer's manner might someday merit the same comment as her money: too much of it. As a matter of fact, if they were being served by footmen, what was the tureen doing in front of her at all?

But at eleven or so, yes, moral illustration, when taken literally, can be dangerous. We were a family of many guests and many, though infrequently regal, dinners at which, since our household was small, I was often allowed up. Time went by while I waited for someone to have his accident, so that I might pridefully watch my mother's aristocratic amends. For months we seemed to feed no one but aunts and uncles; I knew my mother too well to think she would waste that sort of high style on them. But at last one of our guests obliged. He was a Dr. Nettel, fresh from a twenty-year stint in Egypt, who had once been one of my mother's suitors—perhaps it was my father's still sardonic eye on him that caused him to drop a fork into a vegetable dish that splattered wide.

To me, seated at my mother's left, all augured well; the cloth was damask only, but the vegetable was beet. I looked at my mother expectantly; when she did nothing I nudged her, pointing to the service dish of beets which, since it was maid's night out and we were short of footmen, reposed, family-style, in front of her. "Don't be ridiculous," she whispered, her lips sealed, her gaze on the horizon.

I had just been through my eighth-grade graduation—"Into thy hands we give the torch"—the noblesse of our house it would seem, rested with me. I crooked my sharp elbow, bending my hand backward from the wrist as if it held a little pinch of something, meanwhile elegantly averting my head, as if to chitchat, toward Dr. Nettel, but since I could think of nothing to say I remained thus, bas-relief—perhaps he thought I was assuming an Egyptian pose just for him. "Stiff neck?" said my father. My mother, knowing better, grabbed for the elbow; absorbed in the mental picture, profile, of myself, I jumped at the touch; between us we upset the ice pitcher. Diversion was thus created, though not as symmetrically as it would have been via beet. Later, before I went to bed, I was whacked. "Because you are so smart," said my mother between whacks, "and because you are absolutely unteachable." She was wrong. I had just learned for sure what I had always suspected—that we were irretrievably middle-class.

Meanwhile, allegory still pursued me, though from another corner. Other girls my age were becoming women, flirts, sirens—at least girls—without trouble, and some avidly; it was my mother's cross that I had to be nagged there inch by recalcitrant inch. Daintiness, my mother said, was its essence; once a woman's daintiness got through to a man, all consummations devoutly to be wished for—such as a trousseau of one's own triple-monogrammed tea napkins—soon followed. To me the word was "daindee," as our German cook crooned it—"Oooh, so daindee!" over anything fancy—and as she looked on her day off, a clumsy veil of white obscuring everything human, excess of starch in the blouse, powder on the neck, fish-net gloves on her honest, corned-beef hands. To me even a bath was an assault on one's boundaries. Cleanliness was hypocrisy, dirt "sincere." Still the other ethic followed me, ruthlessly inserted in my ear along with the morning and evening soapings, and always with some elaboration peculiar to my mother—witness her divertissement on the Safety Pin.

I belong to the tail end of the button-traumaed generation. The embarrassments of the zipper-reared are quite otherwise—gaps in the memory or the metal, a fear of being locked in. We lived in the opposite fear of—the very words still have a blush and a hush to them—things "dropping down." Camisoles, panties and petticoats, even when snapped or hook-and-eyed, still required ceaseless vigilance with the needle—and thread was fallible, not nylon. Hence the reign of the safety pin, now used only by cleaners and babies. But the protocol of its use was strict. Emergency supply was always in the purse—in my mother's a chain of small gold ones. In case of "accident" one retired somewhere—to the washroom at Wanamaker's for instance—pinned "things up" and rushed home in a pink state of guilt, praying all the while that one would not be knocked down by a car on the way. For the core of the ethic—known, as I found later, to almost every girl of the era—was: "What if you are rushed suddenly to the hospital, and *there they discover . . . ?*" Dream sequences often finished the line, sung above our shrinking forms by hosts of angelic interns forever lost to us: "She has a safety pin in her corset cover!" The worst offense, of course, against sense as well as neatness, was to start the day or the journey already pinned. Hence my mother's variation, known to me always as The Gentleman from Philadelphia.

There was once a girl who was being courted by such a gentleman. Whether there was any significance in his origin, I don't know; perhaps—this being the unsolicited detail with which my mother often fleshed a fable—he just was. *She* was one of those girls (not unknown to me) who were hastily groomed on the surface, at the cost of squalor below. For a while, said my mother, the girl was able to string him along. But, said she, you can't string them along forever—tangentially I tag this as the single allusion she ever made to sex. There came a day when he arrived with intent to propose. It was a warm occasion; the girl was wearing a peekaboo blouse. Perhaps it was warm enough, say, for him to take off his driving goggles and lean closer. Anyway, just as he was about to declare . . . he saw that her shoulder strap was attached with—you've got it. The gentleman went back where he came from. And the girl is single yet.

It has since struck me that she was well shet of him. But at the time—"*Now* do you see?" said my mother, and I mumbled back, "Yerse."

In time of course, through vanity and the sly connivance of the lingerie-makers, I became as "insincere" as any other "nice" woman, although I never quite convinced my mother of it—or myself. "Fine feathers, *on top,*" she would greet a new costume of mine, and sure enough, within minutes, some detail of my toilette would mysteriously unravel. I scrubbed my wedding ring until some of the stones fell out, because she had a habit of murmuring, "Dirty diamonds," whenever she saw an overdressed woman, and I primped for hospital visits as courtesans once may have for their levées. Wanamaker's was torn down, but I sometimes still dreamed myself in its washroom, standing there with the top button gone from my skirt waistband, holding one gaunt safety pin the size of a salmon's skeleton. And I never was able to look a real safety pin straight in its fishy, faintly libidinous eye.

But now—let us return to that table in London. There sit the ladies, swan-necked and squinting—what does the slightly piscine shape of their squint remind me of?—at me. And there, somewhat blue-lawed about the jowl at the very plurality of the situation, sit the men. And me—what I am thinking? As any woman would be, of course, of what I have on underneath. Being me, I am also thinking that I am after all the child, at last the Good Child of my mother, and that the scene before me—although of course she could not possibly countenance it—is the accident we have both been waiting for all my life.

For what I happen to have on underneath—nothing more of course, or less, than what thousands of Rockefeller Center secretaries, window mannequins and ladies out for the evening in Rochester, Elmira and Binghamton are wearing—is a La Belle Hélène Walzette, Model 11A56, Merrie Widowe Waiste Pincher, nyl. lce. blk., size 36 B. Edwardian it may be, but not in execution; no amount of wine will unravel me—Seventh Avenue expertise has machine-tooled me into it and only the hotel chambermaid will get me out. And its modesty is unimpeachable—is, in fact, Mail Order. This, indeed, is the accident. For what I had ordered, in the rush before sailing, was the nyl. lce. wht.—in the catalogue very daindee, with the usual sprig of mashed ribbon rosebuds in the décolletage. But what I have got on—sent me by one of the Eumenides brooding darkly in Best's warehouse—is the blk. And the blk. is not with rosebuds. Blissfully I feel, beneath my sweater, what it *is* with—something to end traumas forever. There, centered where once button or pin might have resided, now lies, locking me in by patents pending, a round red cabochon glass jewel about the size of a nickel, La Belle Hélène's star ruby clasp, my order of merit, winking rosy and waiting for the light.

Or is it? Dare I? I look heavenward, seeing at first only a dim, brackish ceiling in St. John's Wood. But in dreams one does not always rehearse only one's anxieties. Sometimes one dreams that one is walking downtown in one's Walzette, and wakes to find—that one is. And better yet—that Mother is watching. Here I am then, I say upwards. See me now, met with my accident just as you warned me, but in what aristocratic company! There sits Lady Catherine, who began it, surrounded by several others who may well count sixteen quarterings, whatever that is, among them—if not all in one. There indeed sits Mrs. Potter Palmer modern version, with her sweater-tureen in her hand. Mother, you were right. And now, if I do what it appears I must, aren't I?

And immediately I am answered. Nothing supernatural about it—if there is any moral to this fable it is that, unbecoming as we at first may seem to our parents, in the end we become them. At the moment, however, I prefer to think that the suggestion comes via the grate, where a piece of nutty slack slides down, sotto voce. *Ask the lady across from you.*

I do so. I tip Frau Ewig a wink toward the others, signaling, "Shall we join them?" She seems larger and redder in the face than when I last noticed her. Not to my entire surprise, she shakes her head imperceptibly. Under my stare her face empurples further. "*Kann nicht!*" she murmurs at last, her lips unmoving; and as her seams stretch with her breathing, I see why—underneath each of her vast arms, a baleful, metallic winking-back. I look the other way. More's the pity! Anthropologist or no, Frau Ewig was reared in Vienna, and I think I know how. Like me. But I don't see how I can help her. Still, a pity that in every apotheosis of the Good Child, there must be, clinging to the bottom of the ladder and gazing upward, a Bad.

My mother's face, up there like a decal through which I can still see the ceiling, is of course seen by no one but me. She has her eyes closed, knowing, as usual, just what I am about to do, and she cannot quite approve this modern ending to her fable. But she also cannot help smiling. Listen to them, the heavenly host, not of angels but of interns, as leaning down with her in the center of the circle they sing it to me *a cappella, con amore* . . . "and now we discover . . . she has got . . ." (soft Gilbertian surprise) "No! She has not! . . . Yes she has, yes she *has,* she has got . . ." *(pianissimo, ma non troppo)* "a roo-oo-ooo-ooooby . . . yes, a ruby, ruby, ruby, ruby, ruby . . . a Star Ruby in her corset cover!"

And as, with my hand bent a little at the wrist, I make my gesture, all the company, leaning forward with interest—and perhaps even my mother—may see that I have.

The Good Deed

Pearl S. Buck

Mr. Pan was worried about his mother. He had been worried about her when she was in China, and now he was worried about her in New York, although he had thought that once he got her out of his ancestral village in the province of Szechuen and safely away from the local bullies, who took over when the distant government fell, his anxieties would be ended. To this end he had risked his own life and paid out large sums of sound American money, and he felt that day when he saw her on the wharf, a tiny, dazed little old woman, in a lavender silk coat and black skirt, that now they would live happily together, he and his wife, their four small children and his beloved mother, in the huge safety of the American city.

It soon became clear, however, that safety was not enough for old Mrs. Pan. She did not even appreciate the fact, which he repeated again and again, that had she remained in the village, she would now have been dead, because she was the widow of the large landowner who had been his father and therefore deserved death in the eyes of the rowdies in power.

Old Mrs. Pan listened to this without reply, but her eyes, looking very large in her small withered face, were haunted with homesickness.

"There are many things worse than death, especially at my age," she replied at last, when again her son reminded her of her good fortune in being where she was.

He became impassioned when she said this. He struck his breast with clenched fists and he shouted, "Could I have forgiven myself if I had allowed you to die? Would the ghost of my father have given me rest?"

"I doubt his ghost would have traveled over such a wide sea," she replied. "That man was always afraid of the water."

Yet there was nothing that Mr. Pan and his wife did not try to do for his mother in order to make her happy. They prepared the food that she had once enjoyed, but she was now beyond the age of pleasure in food, and she had no appetite. She touched one dish and another with the ends of her ivory chopsticks, which she had brought with her from her home, and she thanked them prettily. "It is all good," she said, "but the water is not the same as our village water; it tastes of metal and not of earth, and so the flavor is not the same. Please allow the children to eat it."

She was afraid of the children. They went to an American school and they spoke English very well and Chinese very badly, and since she could speak no English, it distressed her to hear her own language maltreated by their careless tongues. For a time she tried to coax them to a few lessons, or she told them stories, to which they were too busy to listen. Instead they preferred to look at the moving pictures in the box that stood on a table in the living room. She gave them up finally and merely watched them contemplatively when they were in the same room with her and was glad when they were gone. She liked her son's wife. She did not understand how there could be a Chinese woman who had never been in China, but such her son's wife was. When her son was away, she could not say to her daughter-in-law, "Do you remember how the willows grew over the gate?" For her son's wife had no such memories. She had grown up here in the city and she did not even hear its noise. At the same time, though she was so foreign, she was very kind to the old lady, and she spoke to her always in a gentle voice, however she might shout at the children, who were often disobedient.

The disobedience of the children was another grief to old Mrs. Pan. She did not understand how it was that four children could all be disobedient, for this meant that they had never been taught to obey their parents and revere their elders, which are the first lessons a child should learn.

"How is it," she once asked her son, "that the children do not know how to obey?"

Mr. Pan had laughed, though uncomfortably. "Here in America the children are not taught as we were in China," he explained.

"But my grandchildren are Chinese nevertheless," old Mrs. Pan said in some astonishment.

"They are always with Americans," Mr. Pan explained. "It is very difficult to teach them."

Old Mrs. Pan did not understand, for Chinese and

Americans are different beings, one on the west side of the sea and one on the east, and the sea is always between. Therefore, why should they not continue to live apart even in the same city? She felt in her heart that the children should be kept at home and taught those things which must be learned, but she said nothing. She felt lonely and there was no one who understood the things she felt and she was quite useless. That was the most difficult thing: she was of no use here. She could not even remember which spout the hot water came from and which brought the cold. Sometimes she turned on one and then the other, until her son's wife came in briskly and said, "Let me, Mother."

So she gave up and sat uselessly all day, not by the window, because the machines and the many people frightened her. She sat where she could not see out; she looked at a few books, and day by day she grew thinner and thinner until Mr. Pan was concerned beyond endurance.

One day he said to his wife, "Sophia, we must do something for my mother. There is no use in saving her from death in our village if she dies here in the city. Do you see how thin her hands are?"

"I have seen," his good young wife said. "But what can we do?"

"Is there no woman you know who can speak Chinese with her?" Mr. Pan asked. "She needs to have someone to whom she can talk about the village and all the things she knows. She cannot talk to you because you can only speak English, and I am too busy making our living to sit and listen to her."

Young Mrs. Pan considered. "I have a friend," she said at last, "a schoolmate whose family compelled her to speak

Chinese. Now she is a social worker here in the city. She visits families in Chinatown and this is her work. I will call her up and ask her to spend some time here so that our old mother can be happy enough to eat again."

"Do so," Mr. Pan said.

That very morning, when Mr. Pan was gone, young Mrs. Pan made the call and found her friend, Lili Yang, and she explained everything to her.

"We are really in very much trouble," she said finally. "His mother is thinner every day, and she is so afraid she will die here. She has made us promise that we will not bury her in foreign soil but will send her coffin back to the ancestral village. We have promised, but can we keep this promise, Lili? Yet I am so afraid, because I think she will die, and Billy will think he must keep his promise and he will try to take the coffin back and then he will be killed. Please help us, Lili."

Lili Yang promised and within a few days she came to the apartment and young Mrs. Pan led her into the inner room, which was old Mrs. Pan's room and where she always sat, wrapped in her satin coat and holding a magazine at whose pictures she did not care to look. She took up the magazine when her daughter-in-law came in, because she did not want to hurt her feelings, but the pictures frightened her. The women looked bold and evil, their bosoms bare, and sometimes they wore only a little silk stuff over their legs and this shocked her. She wondered that her son's wife would put such a magazine into her hands, but she did not ask questions. There would have been no end to them had she once begun, and the ways of foreigners did not interest her. Most of the time she sat silent and still, her head sunk on her breast, dreaming of the village, the big house there where she and her husband had lived together with his parents and where their children were born. She knew that the village had fallen into the hands of their enemies and that strangers lived in the house, but she hoped even so that the land was tilled. All that she remembered was the way it had been when she was a young woman and before the evil had come to pass.

She heard now her daughter-in-law's voice, "Mother, this is a friend. She is Miss Lili Yang. She has come to see you."

Old Mrs. Pan remembered her manners. She tried to rise but Lili took her hands and begged her to keep seated.

"You must not rise to one so much younger," she exclaimed.

Old Mrs. Pan lifted her head. "You speak such good Chinese!"

"I was taught by my parents," Lili said. She sat down on a chair near the old lady.

Mrs. Pan leaned forward and put her hand on Lili's knee. "Have you been in our own country?" she asked eagerly.

Lili shook her head. "That is my sorrow. I have not and I want to know about it. I have come here to listen to you tell me."

"Excuse me," young Mrs. Pan said, "I must prepare the dinner for the family."

She slipped away so that the two could be alone and old Mrs. Pan looked after her sadly. "She never wishes to hear; she is always busy."

"You must remember in this country we have no servants," Lili reminded her gently.

"Yes," old Mrs. Pan said, "and why not? I have told my son it is not fitting to have my daughter-in-law cooking and washing in the kitchen. We should have at least three servants: one for me, one for the children and one to clean and cook. At home we had many more but here we have only a few rooms."

Lili did not try to explain. "Everything is different here and let us not talk about it," she said. "Let us talk about your home and the village. I want to know how it looks and what goes on there."

Old Mrs. Pan was delighted. She smoothed the gray satin of her coat as it lay on her knees and she began.

"You must know that our village lies in a wide valley from which the mountains rise as sharply as tiger's teeth."

"Is it so?" Lili said, making a voice of wonder.

"It is, and the village is not a small one. On the contrary, the walls encircle more than one thousand souls, all of whom are relatives of our family,"

"A large family," Lili said.

"It is," old Mrs. Pan said, "and my son's father was the head of it. We lived in a house with seventy rooms. It was in the midst of the village. We had gardens in the courtyards. My own garden contained also a pool wherein are aged goldfish, very fat. I fed them millet and they knew me."

"How amusing." Lili saw with pleasure that the old lady's cheeks were faintly pink and that her large beautiful eyes were beginning to shine and glow. "And how many years did you live there, Ancient One?"

"I went there as a bride. I was seventeen." She looked at Lili, questioning, "How old are you?"

Lili smiled, somewhat ashamed. "I am twenty-seven."

Mrs. Pan was shocked. "Twenty-seven? But my son's wife called you Miss."

"I am not married," Lili confessed.

Mrs. Pan was instantly concerned. "How is this?" she asked. "Are your parents dead?"

"They are dead," Lili said, "but it is not their fault that I am not married."

Old Mrs. Pan would not agree to this. She shook her head with decision. "It is the duty of the parents to arrange the marriage of the children. When death approached, they should have attended to this for you. Now who is left to perform the task? Have you brothers?"

"No," Lili said, "I am an only child. But please don't worry yourself, Madame Pan. I am earning my own living and there are many young women like me in this country."

Old Mrs. Pan was dignified about this. "I cannot be responsible for what other persons do, but I must be responsible for my own kind," she declared. "Allow me to know the names of the suitable persons who can arrange your marriage. I will stand in the place of your mother. We are all in a foreign country now and we must keep together and the old must help the young in these important matters."

Lili was kind and she knew that Mrs. Pan meant kindness. "Dear Madame Pan," she said. "Marriage in America is very different from marriage in China. Here the young people choose their own mates."

"Why do you not choose, then?" Mrs. Pan said with some spirit.

Lili Yang looked abashed. "Perhaps it would be better for me to say that only the young men choose. It is they who must ask the young women."

"What do the young women do?" Mrs. Pan inquired.

"They wait," Lili confessed.

"And if they are not asked?"

"They continue to wait," Lili said gently.

"How long?" Mrs. Pan demanded.

"As long as they live."

Old Mrs. Pan was profoundly shocked. "Do you tell me that there is no person who arranges such matters when it is necessary?"

"Such an arrangement is not thought of here," Lili told her.

"And they allow their women to remain unmarried?" Mrs. Pan exclaimed. "Are there also sons who do not marry?"

"Here men do not marry unless they wish to do so."

Mrs. Pan was even more shocked. "How can this be?" she asked. "Of course, men will not marry unless they are compelled to do so to provide grandchildren for the family. It is necessary to make laws and create customs so that a man who will not marry is denounced as an unfilial son and one who does not fulfill his duty to his ancestors."

"Here the ancestors are forgotten and parents are not important," Lili said unwillingly.

"What a country is this," Mrs. Pan exclaimed. "How can such a country endure?"

Lili did not reply. Old Mrs. Pan had unknowingly touched upon a wound in her heart. No man had ever asked her to marry him. Yet above all else she would like to be married and to have children. She was a good social worker, and the head of the Children's Bureau sometimes told her that he would not know what to do without her and she must never leave them, for then there would be no one to serve the people in Chinatown. She did not wish to leave except to be married, but how could she find a husband? She looked down at her hands, clasped in her lap, and thought that if she had been in her own country, if her father had not come here as a young man and married here, she would have been in China and by now the mother of many children. Instead what would become of her? She would grow older and older, and twenty-seven was already old, and at last hope must die. She knew several American girls quite well; they liked her, and she knew that they faced the same fate. They, too, were waiting. They tried very hard; they went in summer to hotels and in winter to ski lodges, where men gathered and were at leisure enough to think about them, and in confidence they told one another of their efforts. They compared their experiences and they asked anxious questions. "Do you think men like talkative women or quiet ones?" "Do you think men like lipstick or none?" Such questions they asked of one another and who could answer them? If a girl succeeded in winning a proposal from a man, then all the other girls envied her and asked her special questions and immediately she became someone above them all, a successful woman. The job which had once been so valuable then became worthless and it was given away easily and gladly. But how could she explain this to old Mrs. Pan?

Meanwhile Mrs. Pan had been studying Lili's face carefully and with thought. This was not a pretty girl. Her face was too flat, and her mouth was large. She looked like a girl from Canton and not from Hangchow or Soochow. But she had nice skin, and her eyes, though small, were kind. She was the sort of girl, Mrs. Pan could see, who would make an excellent wife and a good mother, but certainly she was one for whom a marriage must be arranged. She was a decent, plain, good girl and, left to herself, Mrs. Pan could predict, nothing at all would happen. She would wither away like a dying flower.

Old Mrs. Pan forgot herself and for the first time since

she had been hurried away from the village without even being allowed to stop and see that the salted cabbage, drying on ropes across the big courtyard, was brought in for the winter. She had been compelled to leave it there and she had often thought of it with regret. She could have brought some with her had she known it was not to be had here. But there it was, and it was only one thing among others that she had left undone. Many people depended upon her and she had left them, because her son compelled her, and she was not used to this idleness that was killing her day by day.

Now as she looked at Lili's kind, ugly face it occurred to her that here there was something she could do. She could find a husband for this good girl, and it would be counted for merit when she went to heaven. A good deed is a good deed, whether one is in China or in America, for the same heaven stretches above all.

She patted Lili's clasped hands. "Do not grieve anymore," she said tenderly. "I will arrange everything."

"I am not grieving," Lili said.

"Of course you are," Mrs. Pan retorted. "I see you are a true woman, and women grieve when they are not wed so that they can have children. You are grieving for your children."

Lili could not deny it. She would have been ashamed to confess to any other person except this old Chinese lady who might have been her grandmother. She bent her head and bit her lip; she let a tear or two fall upon her hands. Then she nodded. Yes, she grieved in the secret places of her heart, in the darkness of the lonely nights, when she thought of the empty future of her life.

"Do not grieve," old Mrs. Pan was saying, "I will arrange it; I will do it."

It was so comforting a murmur that Lili could not bear it. She said, "I came to comfort you, but it is you who comfort me." Then she got up and went out of the room quickly because she did not want to sob aloud. She was unseen, for young Mrs. Pan had gone to market and the children were at school, and Lili went away telling herself that it was all absurd, that an old woman from the middle of China who could not speak a word of English would not be able to change this American world, even for her.

Old Mrs. Pan could scarcely wait for her son to come home at noon. She declined to join the family at the table, saying that she must speak to her son first.

When he came in, he saw at once that she was changed. She held up her head and she spoke to him sharply when he came into the room, as though it was her house and not his in which they now were.

"Let the children eat first," she commanded, "I shall need time to talk with you and I am not hungry."

He repressed his inclination to tell her that he was hungry and that he must get back to the office. Something in her look made it impossible for him to be disobedient to her. He went away and gave the children direction and then returned.

"Yes, my mother," he said, seating himself on a small and uncomfortable chair.

Then she related to him with much detail and repetition what had happened that morning; she declared with indignation that she had never before heard of a country where no marriages were arranged for the young, leaving to them the most important event of their lives and that at a time when their judgment was still unripe, and a mistake could bring disaster upon the whole family.

"Your own marriage," she reminded him, "was arranged by your father with great care, our two families knowing each other well. Even though you and my daughter-in-law were distant in this country, yet we met her parents through a suitable go-between, and her uncle here stood in her father's place, and your father's friend in place of your father, and so it was all done according to custom though so far away."

Mr. Pan did not have the heart to tell his mother that he and his wife Sophia had fallen in love first, and then, out of kindness to their elders, had allowed the marriage to be arranged for them as though they were not in love, and as though, indeed, they did not know each other. They were both young people of heart, and although it would have been much easier to be married in the American fashion, they considered their elders.

"What has all this to do with us now, my mother?" he asked.

"This is what is to do," she replied with spirit. "A nice, ugly girl of our own people came here today to see me. She is twenty-seven years old and she is not married. What will become of her?"

"Do you mean Lili Yang?" her son asked.

"I do," she replied. "When I heard that she has no way of being married because, according to the custom of this country, she must wait for a man to ask her—"

Old Mrs. Pan broke off and gazed at her son with horrified eyes.

"What now?" he asked.

"Suppose the only man who asks is one who is not at all suitable?"

"It is quite possible that it often happens thus," her son said, trying not to laugh.

"Then she has no choice," old Mrs. Pan said indignantly. "She can only remain unmarried or accept one who is unsuitable."

"Here she has no choice," Mr. Pan agreed, "unless she is very pretty, my mother, when several men may ask and then she has a choice." It was on the tip of his tongue to tell how at least six young men had proposed to his Sophia, thereby distressing him continually until he was finally chosen, but he thought better of it. Would it not be very hard to explain so much to his old mother, and could she understand? He doubted it. Nevertheless, he felt it necessary at least to make one point.

"Something must be said for the man also, my mother. Sometimes he asks a girl who will not have him, because she chooses another, and then his sufferings are intense. Unless he wishes to remain unmarried he must ask a second girl, who is not the first one. Here also is some injustice."

Old Mrs. Pan listened to this attentively and then declared, "It is all barbarous. Certainly it is very embarrassing to be compelled to speak of these matters, man and woman, face to face. They should be spared; others should speak for them."

She considered for a few seconds and then she said with fresh indignation, "And what woman can change the appearance her ancestors have given her? Because she is not pretty is she less a woman? Are not her feelings like any woman's; is it not right to have husband and home and children? It is well-known that men have no wisdom in such matters; they believe that a woman's face is all she has, forgetting that everything else is the same. They gather about the pretty woman, who is surfeited with them, and leave alone the good woman. And I do not know why heaven has created ugly women always good but so it is, whether here or in our own country, but what man is wise enough to know that? Therefore his wife should be chosen for him, so that the family is not burdened with his follies."

Mr. Pan allowed all this to be said and then he inquired, "What is on your mind, my mother?"

Old Mrs. Pan leaned toward him and lifted her forefinger. "This is what I command you to do for me, my son. I myself will find a husband for this good girl of our people. She is helpless and alone. But I know no one; I am a stranger, and I must depend upon you. In your business there must be young men. Inquire of them and see who stands for them, so that we can arrange a meeting between them and me; I will stand for the girl's mother. I promised it."

Now Mr. Pan laughed heartily. "Oh, my mother!" he cried. "You are too kind, but it cannot be done. They would laugh at me, and do you believe that Lili Yang herself would like such an arrangement? I think she would not. She has been in America too long."

Old Mrs. Pan would not yield, however, and in the end he was compelled to promise that he would see what he could do. Upon this promise she consented to eat her meal, and he led her out, her right hand resting upon his left wrist. The children were gone and they had a quiet meal together, and after it she said she felt that she would sleep. This was good news, for she had not slept well since she came, and young Mrs. Pan led her into the bedroom and helped her to lie down and placed a thin quilt over her.

When young Mrs. Pan went back to the small dining

room where her husband waited to tell her what his mother had said, she listened thoughtfully.

"It is absurd," her husband said, "but what shall we do to satisfy my mother? She sees it as a good deed if she can find a husband for Lili Yang."

Here his wife surprised him. "I can see some good in it myself," she declared. "I have often felt for Lili. It is a problem, and our mother is right to see it as such. It is not only Lili—it is a problem here for all young women, especially if they are not pretty." She looked quizzically at her husband for a moment and then said, "I too used to worry when I was very young, lest I should not find a husband for myself. It is a great burden for a young woman. It would be nice to have someone else arrange the matter."

"Remember," he told her, "how often in the old country the wrong men are arranged for and how often the young men leave home because they do not like the wives their parents choose for them."

"Well, so do they here," she said pertly. "Divorce, divorce, divorce!"

"Come, come," he told her. "It is not so bad."

"It is very bad for women," she insisted. "When there is divorce here, then she is thrown out of the family. The ties are broken. But in the old country, it is the man who leaves home and the woman stays on, for she is still the daughter-in-law and her children will belong to the family, and however far away the man wants to go, she has her place and she is safe."

Mr. Pan looked at his watch. "It is late and I must go to the office."

"Oh, your office," young Mrs. Pan said in an uppish voice, "what would you do without it?"

They did not know it but their voices roused old Mrs. Pan in the bedroom, and she opened her eyes. She could not understand what they said for they spoke in English, but she understood that there was an argument. She sat up on the bed to listen, then she heard the door slam and she knew her son was gone. She was about to lie down again when it occurred to her that it would be interesting to look out of the window to the street and see what young men there were coming to and fro. One did not choose men from the street, of course, but still she could see what their looks were.

She got up and tidied her hair and tottered on her small feet over to the window and opening the curtains a little she gazed into the street really for the first time since she came. She was pleased to see many Chinese men, some of them young. It was still not late, and they loitered in the sunshine before going back to work, talking and laughing and looking happy. It was interesting to her to watch them, keeping in mind Lili Yang and thinking to herself that it might be this one or that one, although still one did not choose men from the street. She stood so long that at last she became tired and she pulled the small chair to the window and kept looking through the parted curtain.

Here her daughter-in-law saw her a little later, when she opened the door to see if her mother-in-law was awake, but she did not speak. She looked at the little satin-clad figure, and went away again, wondering why it was that the old lady found it pleasant today to look out of the window when every other day she had refused the same pleasure.

It became a pastime for old Mrs. Pan to look out of the window every day from then on. Gradually she came to know some of the young men, not by name but by their faces and by the way they walked by her window, never, of course looking up at her, until one day a certain young man did look up and smile. It was a warm day, and she had asked that the window be opened, which until now she had not allowed, for fear she might be assailed by the foreign winds and made ill. Today, however, was near to summer, she felt the room airless and she longed for freshness.

After this the young man habitually smiled when he passed or nodded his head. She was too old to have it mean anything but courtesy and so bit by bit she allowed herself to make a gesture of her hand in return. It was evident that he belonged in a china shop across the narrow street. She watched him go in and come out; she watched him stand at the door in his shirt sleeves on a fine day and talk and laugh, showing, as she observed, strong white teeth set off by two gold ones. Evidently he made money. She did not believe he was married, for she saw an old man who must be his father, who smoked a water pipe, and now and then an elderly woman, perhaps his mother, and a younger brother, but there was no young woman.

She began after some weeks of watching to fix upon this young man as a husband for Lili. But who could be the go-between except her own son?

She confided her plans one night to him, and, as always, he listened to her with courtesy and concealed amusement. "But the young man, my mother, is the son of Mr. Lim, who is the richest man on our street."

"That is nothing against him," she declared.

"No, but he will not submit to an arrangement, my mother. He is a college graduate. He is only spending the summer at home in the shop to help his father."

"Lili Yang has also been to school."

"I know, my mother, but, you see, the young man will want to choose his own wife, and it will not be someone who looks like Lili Yang. It will be someone who—"

He broke off and made a gesture which suggested curled hair, a fine figure and an air. Mrs. Pan watched him with disgust. "You are like all these other men, though you are my son," she said, and dismissed him sternly.

Nevertheless, she thought over what he had said when she went back to the window. The young man was standing on the street picking his fine teeth and laughing at friends who passed, the sun shining on his glistening black hair. It was true he did not look at all obedient; it was perhaps true that he was no more wise than other men and so saw only what a girl's face was. She wished that she could speak to him, but that, of course, was impossible. Unless—

She drew in a long breath. Unless she went downstairs and out into that street and crossed it and entered the shop, pretending that she came to buy something! If she did this, she could speak to him. But what would she say, and who would help her cross the street? She did not want to tell her son or her son's wife, for they would suspect her and laugh. They teased her often even now about her purpose, and Lili was so embarrassed by their laughter that she did not want to come anymore.

Old Mrs. Pan reflected on the difficulty of her position as a lady in a barbarous and strange country. Then she thought of her eldest grandson, Johnnie. On Saturday, when her son was at his office and her son's wife was at the market, she would coax Johnnie to lead her across the street to the china shop; she would pay him some money, and in the shop she would say she was looking for two bowls to match some that had been broken. It would be an expedition, but she might speak to the young man and tell him—what should she tell him? That must first be planned.

This was only Thursday and she had only two days to prepare. She was very restless during those two days, and she could not eat. Mr. Pan spoke of a doctor, whom she indignantly refused to see, because he was a man and also because she was not ill. But Saturday came at last and everything came about as she planned. Her son went away, and then her son's wife, and she crept downstairs with much effort to the sidewalk where her grandson was playing marbles and beckoned him to her. The child was terrified to see her there and came at once, and she pressed a coin into his palm and pointed across the street with her cane.

"Lead me there," she commanded, and, shutting her eyes tightly, she put her hand on his shoulder and allowed him to lead her to the shop. Then to her dismay he left her and ran back to play and she stood wavering on the threshold, feeling dizzy, and the young man saw her and came hurrying toward her. To her joy he spoke good Chinese, and the words fell sweetly upon her old ears.

"Ancient One, Ancient One," he chided her kindly. "Come in and sit down. It is too much for you."

He led her inside the cool, dark shop and she sat down on a bamboo chair.

"I came to look for two bowls," she said faintly.

"Tell me the pattern and I will get them for you," he said. "Are they blue willow pattern or the thousand flowers?"

"Thousand flowers," she said in the same faint voice, "but I do not wish to disturb you."

"I am here to be disturbed," he replied with the utmost courtesy.

He brought out some bowls and set them on a small table before her and she fell to talking with him. He was very pleasant; his rather large face was shining with kindness and he laughed easily. Now that she saw him close, she was glad to notice that he was not too handsome; his nose and mouth were big, and he had big hands and feet.

"You look like a countryman," she said. "Where is your ancestral home?"

"It is in the province of Shantung," he replied, "and there are not many of us here."

"That explains why you are so tall," she said. "These people from Canton are small. We of Szechuen are also big and our language is yours. I cannot understand the people of Canton."

From this they fell to talking of their own country, which he had never seen, and she told him about the village and how her son's father had left it many years ago to do business here in this foreign country and how he had sent for their son and then how she had been compelled to flee because the country was in fragments and torn between many leaders. When she had told him this much, she found herself telling him how difficult it was to live here and how strange the city was to her and how she would never have looked out of the window had it not been for the sake of Lili Yang.

"Who is Lili Yang?" he asked.

Old Mrs. Pan did not answer him directly. That would not have been suitable. One does not speak of a reputable young woman to any man, not even one as good as this one. Instead she began a long speech about the virtues of young women who were not pretty, and how beauty in a woman made virtue unlikely, and how a woman not beautiful was always grateful to her husband and did not consider that she had done him a favor by the marriage, but rather that it was he who conferred the favor, so that she served him far better than she could have done were she beautiful.

To all this the young man listened, his small eyes twinkling with laughter.

"I take it that this Lili Yang is not beautiful," he said.

Old Mrs. Pan looked astonished. "I did not say so," she replied with spirit. "I will not say she is beautiful and I will not say she is ugly. What is beautiful to one is not so to another. Suppose you see her sometime for yourself, and then we will discuss it."

"Discuss what?" he demanded.

"Whether she is beautiful."

Suddenly she felt that she had come to a point and that she had better go home. It was enough for the first visit. She chose two bowls and paid for them and while he wrapped them up she waited in silence, for to say too much is worse than to say too little.

When the bowls were wrapped, the young man said courteously, "Let me lead you across the street, Ancient One."

So, putting her right hand on his left wrist, she let him lead her across and this time she did not shut her eyes, and she came home again feeling that she had been a long way and had accomplished much. When her daughter-in-law came home she said quite easily, "I went across the street and bought these two bowls."

Young Mrs. Pan opened her eyes wide. "My mother, how could you go alone?"

"I did not go alone," old Mrs. Pan said tranquilly. "My grandson led me across and young Mr. Lim brought me back."

Each had spoken in her own language with helpful gestures.

Young Mrs. Pan was astonished and she said no more until her husband came home, when she told him. He laughed a great deal and said, "Do not interfere with our old one. She is enjoying herself. It is good for her."

But all the time he knew what his mother was doing and he joined in it without her knowledge. That is to say, he telephoned the same afternoon from his office to Miss Lili Yang, and when she answered, he said, "Please come and see my old mother again. She asks for you every day. Your visit did her much good."

Lili Yang promised, not for today but for a week hence, and when Mr. Pan went home he told his mother carelessly, as though it were nothing, that Lili Yang had called him up to say she was coming again next week.

Old Mrs. Pan heard this with secret excitement. She had not gone out again, but every day young Mr. Lim nodded to her and smiled, and once he sent her a small gift of fresh ginger root. She made up her mind slowly but she made it up well. When Lili Yang came again, she would ask her to take her to the china shop, pretending that she wanted to buy something, and she would introduce the two to each other; that much she would do. It was too much, but, after all, these were modern times, and this was a barbarous country, where it did not matter greatly whether the old customs were kept or not. The important thing was to find a husband for Lili, who was already twenty-seven years old.

So it all came about, and when Lili walked into her

room the next week, while the fine weather still held, old Mrs. Pan greeted her with smiles. She seized Lili's small hand and noticed that the hand was very soft and pretty, as the hands of most plain-faced girls are, the gods being kind to such women and giving them pretty bodies when they see that ancestors have not bestowed pretty faces.

"Do not take off your foreign hat," she told Lili. "I wish to go across the street to that shop and buy some dishes as a gift for my son's wife. She is very kind to me."

Lili Yang was pleased to see the old lady so changed and cheerful and in all innocence she agreed and they went across the street and into the shop. Today there were customers, and old Mr. Lim was there too, as well as his son. He was a tall, withered man, and he wore a small beard under his chin. When he saw old Mrs. Pan he stopped what he was doing and brought her a chair to sit upon while she waited. As soon as his customer was gone, he introduced himself, saying that he knew her son.

"My son has told me of your honored visit last week," he said. "Please come inside and have some tea. I will have my son bring the dishes, and you can look at them in quiet. It is too noisy here."

She accepted his courtesy, and in a few minutes young Mr. Lim came back to the inner room with the dishes while a servant brought tea.

Old Mrs. Pan did not introduce Lili Yang, for it was not well to embarrass a woman, but young Mr. Lim boldly introduced himself, in English.

"Are you Miss Lili Yang?" he asked. "I am James Lim."

"How did you know my name?" Lili asked, astonished.

"I have met you before, not face to face, but through Mrs. Pan," he said, his small eyes twinkling. "She has told me more about you than she knows."

Lili blushed. "Mrs. Pan is so old-fashioned," she murmured. "You must not believe her."

"I shall only believe what I see for myself," he said gallantly. He looked at her frankly and Lili kept blushing. Old Mrs. Pan had not done her justice, he thought. The young woman had a nice, round face, the sort of face he liked. She was shy, and he liked that also. It was something new.

Meanwhile old Mrs. Pan watched all this with amazement. So this was the way it was: The young man began speaking immediately, and the young woman blushed. She wished that she knew what they were saying but perhaps it was better that she did not know.

She turned to old Mr. Lim, who was sitting across the square table sipping tea. At least here she could do her duty. "I hear your son is not married," she said in a tentative way.

"Not yet," Mr. Lim said. "He wants first to finish learning how to be a Western doctor."

"How old is he?" Mrs. Pan inquired.

"He is twenty-eight. It is very old but he did not make up his mind for some years, and the learning is long."

"Miss Lili Yang is twenty-seven," Mrs. Pan said in the same tentative voice.

The young people were still talking in English and not listening to them. Lili was telling James Lim about her work and about old Mrs. Pan. She was not blushing anymore; she had forgotten, it seemed, that he was a young man and she a young woman. Suddenly she stopped and blushed again. A woman was supposed to let a man talk about himself, not about her.

"Tell me about your work," she said. "I wanted to be a doctor, too, but it cost too much."

"I can't tell you here," he said. "There are customers waiting in the shop and it will take a long time. Let me come to see you, may I? I could come on Sunday when the shop is closed. Or we could take a ride on one of the riverboats. Will you? The weather is so fine."

"I have never been on a riverboat," she said. "It would be delightful."

She forgot her work and remembered that he was a young man and that she was a young woman. She liked his big face and the way his black hair fell back from his forehead and she knew that a day on the river could be a day in heaven.

The customers were getting impatient. They began to call out and he got up. "Next Sunday," he said in a low voice. "Let's start early. I'll be at the wharf at nine o'clock."

"We do not know each other," she said, reluctant and yet eager. Would he think she was too eager?

He laughed. "You see my respectable father, and I know old Mrs. Pan very well. Let them guarantee us."

He hurried away, and old Mrs. Pan said immediately to Lili, "I have chosen these four dishes. Please take them and have them wrapped. Then we will go home."

Lili obeyed, and when she was gone, old Mrs. Pan leaned toward old Mr. Lim.

"I wanted to get her out of the way," she said in a low and important voice. "Now, while she is gone, what do you say? Shall we arrange a match? We do not need a go-between. I stand as her mother, let us say, and you are his father. We must have their horoscopes read, of course, but just between us, it looks as though it is suitable, does it not?"

Mr. Lim wagged his head. "If you recommend her, Honorable Old Lady, why not?"

Why not, indeed? After all, things were not so different here, after all.

"What day is convenient for you?" she asked.

"Shall we say Sunday?" old Mr. Lim suggested.

"Why not?" she replied. "All days are good, when one performs a good deed, and what is better than to arrange a marriage?"

"Nothing is better," old Mr. Lim agreed. "Of all good deeds under heaven, it is the best."

They fell silent, both pleased with themselves, while they waited.

Acknowledgments

"Fenstad's Mother" by Charles Baxter from *A Relative Stranger: Stories by Charles Baxter.* Copyright © 1990 by *The Atlantic.* Reprinted by permission of the author and W. W. Norton & Company, Inc.

"The Augsburg Chalk Circle" by Bertolt Brecht from *Bertolt Brecht: Short Stories 1921–1946.* Copyright © 1949 by Gebruder Weiss Verlag. Reprinted by permission of Methuen Inc.

"The Good Deed" from *The Good Deed and Other Stories* by Pearl S. Buck. Copyright © 1953, 1962, 1963, 1969 by Pearl S. Buck. Reprinted by permission of HarperCollins Publishers, Inc.

"Songs My Mother Taught Me" by Hortense Calisher from *The Collected Stories of Hortense Calisher.* Reprinted by permission of Donadio & Ashworth, Inc. Copyright © 1959, 1975 by Hortense Calisher.

Acknowledgments

"Another Marvelous Thing" from *Another Marvelous Thing* by Laurie Colwin. Copyright © 1984, 1986 by Laurie Colwin. Reprinted by permission of Donadio & Ashworth, Inc. Originally appeared in *The New Yorker.*

"Groom Service" from *Working Men* by Michael Dorris. Copyright © 1989 by Michael Dorris. Reprinted by permission of Henry Holt & Co., Inc.

"The Leap" by Louise Erdrich. Copyright © 1990 by Louise Erdrich. Originally appeared in *Harper's Magazine.* A substantially altered form of this story is incorporated into Louise Erdrich's forthcoming novel *Tales of Burning Love.* Reprinted by permission of the author.

"Mothers and Daughters" from *Through the Window: My Thirty Years with the Chimpanzees of Gombe* by Jane Goodall. Copyright © 1990 by Soko Publications Limited. Reprinted by permission of Houghton Mifflin Co. All rights reserved.

"Happiness" from *Selected Stories of Mary Lavin.* Reprinted by permission of the author. Copyright © 1964, 1981 by Mary Lavin.

"Gravity" from *A Place I've Never Been* by David Leavitt. Copyright © 1990 by David Leavitt. Used by permission of Viking Penguin, a division of Penguin Books USA Inc.

"The Shepherd's Wife" by William Maxwell from *The Old Man at the Railroad Crossing and Other Tales.* Copyright © 1958 by William Maxwell. Reprinted by permission of Wylie, Aitken & Stone. Originally appeared in *The New Yorker.*

"My Oedipus Complex" by Frank O'Connor from *Collected Stories by Frank O'Connor.* Copyright © 1950 by Frank O'Connor. Reprinted by permission of Alfred A. Knopf, Inc., and the Joan Daves Agency.

"Women and Children First" by Francine Prose. Copyright © 1987 by Francine Prose. First appeared in *The New Yorker.* Reprinted by permission of Georges Borchardt, Inc.

"Everyday Use" from *In Love and Trouble* by Alice Walker. Copyright © 1973 by Alice Walker. Reprinted by permission of Harcourt Brace and Company.